"He needs you, Teresa."

She swiped at her face. "He needs help. I'll give you that. But it can't be from me, Dennis. I can't do it. He needs something more than what I can give him."

"Maybe so. But right now you're all he has. Something has gotten under Benny's skin. I don't know what it is, and he's not talking about it. But I know that I need you, Teresa. He needs you."

When Teresa lifted her chin, something had changed in her expression. She was closed off just as she had been when he first made his request this afternoon.

"I'm sorry, Dennis, but I just can't help you here. I'll only make things worse."

Turning on her heels, she escaped into the cold darkness. Dennis didn't bother to go after her.

He turned and strode back through the clinic doors, making a silent prayer to the Lord to find the answers. For all their sakes.

Books by Lisa Mondello

Love Inspired

Fresh-Start Family
In a Doctor's Arms

Love Inspired Suspense

Cradle of Secrets
Her Only Protector
Yuletide Protector

LISA MONDELLO

Lisa's love of writing romance started early when she penned her first romance novel (a full fifty-eight pages long, but who's counting) at the age of ten. She then went on to write a mystery script that impressed her sixth-grade teacher so much he let her and her friends present it as a play to the whole grade. There was no stopping her after that! After studying sound recording technology in college and managing a Boston rock band for four years, she settled down with her husband and raised a family. Although she's held many jobs through the years, ranging from working with musicians and selling kitchen and catering tools to teaching first and second graders with special needs how to read and write, her love of writing has always stayed in the forefront, and she is now a full-time freelance writer. In many ways writing for Steeple Hill Books feels like coming home. Lisa lives in western Massachusetts with her husband, four children (who never cease to amaze her as they grow), a very pampered beagle and a rag doll cat who thinks she owns them all.

In a Doctor's Arms
Lisa Mondello

Steeple
Hill®

Published by Steeple Hill Books™

STEEPLE HILL BOOKS

Steeple
Hill®

Recycling programs
for this product may
not exist in your area.

ISBN-13: 978-0-373-81537-1

IN A DOCTOR'S ARMS

www.SteepleHill.com

Printed in U.S.A.

Heal me, O Lord, and I shall be healed; save me, and I shall be saved, for You are my praise.
—*Jeremiah* 17:14

I have been blessed with many things in my life, including wonderful friendships. This book is dedicated with hugs to my dear friend Cathy McDavid. My life is so much richer having you in it.

Chapter One

New Year's Day

"I didn't know who else to come to. I really need your help."

Teresa Morales listened to Dr. Dennis Harrington's words as she sat curled up on the soft beige sofa in the lodge at the Stockington Falls Mountain Ski Resort. The fire in the huge granite fireplace in the center of the room was burning hot—almost too hot for her comfort. Or maybe that was just her anxiety kicking in. This was supposed to be her vacation. No one was supposed to need her help here.

She bookmarked the page in the book she had been reading before Dennis's abrupt arrival and closed it, setting it aside on the end table. With a swift motion, she untangled one long leg out from underneath her and brusquely hit her bare feet to the wide pine floor with a dull thud. If this was Dennis's idea of a joke, she wasn't laughing.

"I'm just a tourist. Why would you need my help?"

"Last night…" His voice trailed off, a stricken look on his face, and Teresa knew he wasn't talking about the New Year's Eve party they'd both attended—or the dance they'd shared. No, he was referring to what had happened afterward—the reason behind the beeper call that had pulled him away from the party after their dance. The horrible car crash on the bridge that had been the only topic of conversation throughout Stockington Falls today.

"I'm not sure you understand how severe the accident that took place last night really was."

"I do," she countered quickly. "I could see the whole awful mess right upstairs from my window after I left the party. And I saw what was left of it once the fog lifted this morning. Anyone with a condo facing the west side of the mountain had to have seen and heard what was going on after midnight."

It was human nature to be curious in the wake of flashing emergency lights and sirens, and she certainly had been. After Dennis had left, she'd returned to her room intending to go to sleep. But the flashing lights below had drawn Teresa to the window. She'd stared wide eyed into the night as the snow fell like ash from the dark sky.

She hadn't been able to bring herself to close the curtains, to shield herself from what little she could see through the snow. Soon after the storm subsided, the flashing red, white and blue lights had screamed out into what had been a festive evening. Dragging herself away from what was happening down in the valley didn't seem right. She'd felt she couldn't leave the window until the last tow truck had pulled away. The last of the vehicles, the one that had plunged into the icy water, had been the last to be towed away.

Five months ago, she probably would have been right out there on the road with the rescue workers. As far as she knew, Dennis's clinic didn't have a psychologist on staff. Though she specialized in dealing with children, with her training and experience, she could have been there for the victims, for their families, helping them cope with the tragedy surrounding them.

At one time, maybe Teresa could have done some good. Her gentle guidance might have made a difference between choosing to deal with painful truths or run from them. Now she was the one who was running—running from the events that had shattered her confidence and from the tormenting truth that she had failed.

He shrugged. "It was a tough night."

She was sure it'd been more than just tough for Dennis. He was the only doctor in town—the clinic that he ran was the only medical facility in nearly fifty miles. He'd probably been up all night tending to the victims of the accident. She'd spent the better part of her time standing there praying to God that the people involved would be okay. Dennis had been down there on the ground making sure of it.

"I don't have to tell you that the accident on the bridge was a bad one. Certainly nothing like I've seen since I've been in Stockington Falls."

"How long is that?"

"Except for med school and the military, my whole life. I don't think I've ever seen so many police cars and ambulances lined up along Abbey Bridge Road."

"What is it you think I can do?" she asked against her better judgment.

"You're a school psychologist. You work with young kids. Two teenagers, both hurt, are among the survivors." Dennis's words hit her square in the chest, and she struggled to keep from showing her reaction.

"I know," Teresa said. "One of them is in a coma. He was airlifted to St. Johnsbury for treatment. A woman in her late twenties was also brought in. Another woman, a young mother, was killed. Her little boy was miraculously saved from the explosion."

Teresa found herself chuckling ironically at the shocked look at Dennis's face, despite the severity of the situation.

"You know as well as I do that it's a small town here, Dennis. The grapevine works fast. All I had to do was walk down here to the lodge for some coffee and I got more than what will probably be in the police report."

"Then you understand why I'd like you to talk with one of the teenage survivors, Benny Dulton, about what happened last night."

Counsel teenagers again? Was he kidding?

"No."

She got to her feet and turned to walk away, but he caught her arm.

"Please just hear me out."

"I don't have to."

"True enough. But there really isn't anyone else I can turn to for this. Stockington Falls doesn't have a child psychologist."

Lord, I can't go through this again. I just can't. She said the words silently as her eyes filled with moisture.

"You said it yourself—Stockington Falls doesn't have a child psychologist. That includes me. I don't live here. I'm just on vacation. For all you know, I could be planning to go back to Connecticut tomorrow," she said.

"You're not leaving, are you?" he said, his face tired from the night before but still registering panic.

"The thought had crossed my mind."

"You can help, Teresa. There isn't anyone else." Dennis sighed. "If there was, I wouldn't be troubling you. Benny needs you, and I know you can help him."

Although she straightened her spine and squared her slender shoulders, Teresa realized it was no use. No matter how tall she tried to stand, her five feet two inches were no match against the tall, muscles-built-for-serious-business Dr. Dennis Harrington.

A slight tremor betrayed her determination as her gaze rolled across the room and then settled on his handsome face. He stood a good eight inches above her. Maybe a bit more. His dark hair was almost black and was clipped short so that hardly a hair fell out of place most of the time. Now it was disheveled, possibly from the rough night of working the emergency room and scrubbing his hand over his head in fatigue or frustration.

Yeah, there had probably been a lot of frustration last night, and it showed in the slight bend of his broad shoulders and the rumpled clothes.

Still, there was something commanding about him, even now, when he was clearly exhausted—possibly something linked to the fact that he'd returned from his tour in Iraq just a little over six months ago.

She could understand why a local teenager in trouble was important to him and why the worried lines on his face were so deep. Unlike last night at the annual New Year's Eve party at the ski lodge, Dennis was here today because of a tragedy.

But despite all that, Teresa stood her ground.

"Do you really think that a few conversations over the past month that I've been in town and a twirl around the dance floor last night give you sufficient information about my professional credentials to make this judgment?"

His lips tilted up ever so slightly, revealing only a hint of the straight white teeth that she knew showed when he had a full-blown smile. She was glad he wasn't smiling fully now. That smile might be enough to melt her resolve.

She blinked her thoughts away from the memory of his smile and was staring up at Dennis Harrington again. She wasn't a schoolgirl with a crush. And she wasn't interested in anything Dennis had to say to her right now.

"I'm afraid you've wasted your time coming here. I no longer counsel children," she said resolutely.

His mouth tightened and he sighed, running a hand through his dark wavy hair. With the motion, his black turtleneck stretched taut against his strong shoulders. She remembered vividly how she'd rested her cheek against those shoulders last night when he'd asked her to dance. He'd seemed so strong. Comforting. She'd relished the feeling while it had lasted. But he wasn't offering support or comfort to her now; instead, he was asking her to give it to a child in need. And that was something she just could not do. Not anymore.

Dennis's expression was far more serious than she'd ever seen. Deep lines marred the corners of his mouth and the creases of his eyes that usually she associated with laugh lines.

"You didn't strike me as the type to walk away from a challenge, Teresa," he said.

His words sliced through her like a jagged blade. It may have been true a few months ago. She'd been dubbed a crusader back then. She'd walked the halls of the high school she'd worked at for ten years with the confidence she was making a difference in the lives of the students who sought her help. However, if Teresa was anything, she was a quick learner. Since then, she'd learned her lessons painfully well.

"You barely know me. How would you know?"

"Some things you just know."

She knotted her arms across her chest. "Have you ever heard of the word *vacation,* Dr. Harrington?"

He shrugged. "Not lately, I'm afraid."

"Well, let me spell it out for you. *V-A-C—*"

"I know fully well how to spell the word, *Ms. Morales,*" he said, putting emphasis on the formal address of her name as his lips tilted into a quick smile and his dark brown eyes lit up with amusement.

"Good. Then I'm sure you'll understand my wanting to get back to enjoying mine."

He nodded, unaffected by her attempt to put him off. "I didn't realize the Hartford school system paid their counselor enough to afford a month-long stay at a prime ski resort like Stockington Falls Mountain."

She snapped her gaze to him, shock rippling through her. "How do you know where I worked? I didn't tell you." She hadn't told anyone. Given the state she'd been in when she'd come to Stockington Falls, it was possible she'd let slip her profession, but Teresa had been very careful not to discuss where she was from. There were too many headlines in the papers that made people curious enough to bring up events she didn't want to talk about.

"The information was all on the medical application you filled out when you came to the clinic." Dennis spoke matter of factly, as if it was a common practice to dig up information on total strangers in Stockington Falls.

He made no apology, obviously comfortable with his tactics to uncover information she'd tried not to reveal to just anyone. But then, she had been the one to supply him with all the necessary information he was using to gain entrance into a place she didn't want to go. He didn't know that she'd had a good reason to want to hide her past. No one in Stockington Falls did.

He sat down on the edge of the sofa, hunching forward with his elbows resting on his thighs. He seemed oblivious to the comings and goings of tourists around them.

"I made a few phone calls this morning. You have an excellent reputation as a child psychologist back home." He paused. "By the way, you've been missed."

Teresa closed her eyes at his tender words. Not long ago a compliment like that would have given her pride. Now she wasn't so sure if it was deserved.

She resumed her stance, folding her arms across her chest, uncomfortable with the knowledge that Dennis had gone to such lengths to learn about her past. Suddenly, Teresa was all too aware of the waitress handing out drinks at the tables in the room, of the tourists and of the maintenance man emptying a garbage can close by. Was everyone looking at her?

No, she was just being paranoid. It was only Dennis who was peering up at her, waiting for a response. How much did he know? She would have preferred having revealed certain things about her past herself—and in her own good time. If at all.

"You had a clinic full of patients last night and an earful about my life this morning." She glanced at the digital clock on the wall by the waitress station, tapping her fingers in a staccato rhythm on her arm. "It's just after noon. My, you've been awfully busy. And on New Year's Day, no less."

"All necessary, I assure you. I didn't come here today to give you a hard time, Teresa. I came here to ask for your help. That's all."

Panic seized her as she thought about the possibility.

Lord, I can't do this. I just can't do it.

"No." She shook her head. Definitely no, she

added silently. She couldn't afford any more mistakes at the risk of children.

Guilt stabbed at her with his heavy sigh and the slight shake of his head.

"I'm sorry, Dennis. Really, I am. But I can't be of any help to you. Not in this case," she said quietly. "Please don't ask me again."

Chapter Two

Dennis was desperate, and despite her obvious interest, he could tell that he wasn't getting through to Teresa just how badly he needed her to help him. Dennis wasn't going to take no for an answer, so he positioned himself on the sofa to argue his point.

A waitress came over to where they were seated and interrupted before he could make his case. "Would either of you like something to eat or drink?"

Dennis started to wave her away, wanting to dive back into their discussion, but Teresa took hold of his hand, stopping him. The contact surprised him. "Look, I barely know you, and even I can tell that you're exhausted," she said to him. "Have you even been home since you left the party last night?" His silence was answer enough. "You should try the coffee here. It's quite good."

He couldn't deny that he was dead on his feet.

Coffee would be good, so Dennis put up two fingers. "Coffees for both of us." He turned to Teresa. "Are you hungry?"

"No, I just had breakfast a little while ago, thank you. But you might want to try the turkey croissant sandwich. If you've been running off nothing but coffee for the past twelve hours, then you need something else in your system."

To the waitress he said, "I'll have the sandwich, too. But can you make it to go?"

When the waitress left, Dennis lifted his dark eyes to look at her. "I feel like I'm chasing you around this topic. Me the doctor and you the psychologist. Can we stop for a second and just talk to each other like two people?"

"I thought that's what we were doing."

"You're closing yourself off, and you started getting so stiff with me as soon as you realized why I'm here. Every time I've seen you over the past month, it's always been so easy to talk to you. Except for today. You look like you're ready to bolt. Why do you keep trying to walk away?"

Teresa hesitated a moment and straightened herself. He knew from past experience that meant the conversation had gotten a little too heavy and she was drawing a firm line between them.

"What you're asking for is beyond what I can give you, Dennis."

"Tell me why."

"No."

Feeling defeated, he rested his chin lazily on his steepled fingers, his elbows propped securely on his thighs.

The waitress was quick with the coffee, much to Dennis's liking. He needed some caffeine in order to make his argument stick.

The warm mug felt good in his hands, and he immediately brought it to his lips for a sip. He drank too quickly, burnt his lip on the liquid and grimaced because of the pain.

"Okay?"

"Fine," he said, placing the cup on the end table without another sip.

"I'm curious how you have the time to come here when you must have a clinic full of patients," she said. "Aren't you the only doctor at the clinic?"

"Yes, but the clinic staff is well trained in dealing with injuries. We have a top-notch trauma unit to deal with all the skiing and snowboarding accidents. No one wants a disaster like this crash to happen, but it's a relief to know that at least we're prepared for it."

If this accident had happened before Dennis had come back from Iraq, before he'd started the clinic…but no, through God's grace that disaster had been averted. The injured had received proper medical care in short order, and lives that might have otherwise been lost had been saved. In spite of the tragedy, there was still that to be thankful for.

"The nearest hospital is over forty-five minutes away," he continued. "Most people with serious injuries get airlifted to St. Johnsbury, like some of the injured from last night's accident, but we're well equipped to handle the rest. I trust my staff. I don't have many full-time people, but the whole staff is on call 24/7, and a situation like this has everyone coming in. Now that the immediate crisis is over, they can keep an eye on things for an hour or so without me. My head nurse Cammie Reynolds has things under control right now. She's a good trauma nurse and nurse practitioner—the best, in fact. I couldn't have sorted out last night without her."

She quirked an eyebrow and seemed to be suppressing a smile. "Then if it is all under control, what's left for me to clean up?"

"Cammie is…" He sighed, choosing his words carefully. "This is a small town, Teresa. Most everyone knew the woman who was killed in last night's accident, including those of us at the clinic. Cammie was her best friend since childhood. The EMT who brought her in had been engaged to her for a few months before they broke up and she married John Peterson." He shrugged. "I even dated her once in high school. This community is like a large family."

Instinctively, Teresa placed her hand on her chest. "It must have been so difficult for all of you then."

"The frenzy of last night made our little emergency room feel much like it did during my residency in Boston and a bit like my time as a military doctor in Iraq after a raid. Except this time we knew everyone involved in the accident. That's not something we're used to experiencing here in Stockington Falls. But once the initial shock wore thin, we all managed to keep our composure and do what we needed to do."

Dennis took a quick sip of coffee. "To make matters even worse, Molly has left a young son."

"Molly?"

"The woman who was killed."

"Oh, I didn't know her name. I feel so sad for that poor boy," she said. "How old is he?"

"Drew is seven. He was in the car at the time of the accident, but somehow, thank God, he managed to escape the truck and make it to shore before the Bronco burst into flames."

"Yes, I heard the staff here talking about that earlier. God was definitely with that little boy."

Teresa's eyes were drawn as if deep in thought,

waging war against what she'd just heard. What the child had seen last night must have been horrific, and the look on Drew's face at the clinic still haunted Dennis hours later.

"How is Drew today?" Teresa asked.

"He'll be fine physically, with time. He's a strong kid. He's got a nasty gash on his head and a broken arm, but he's alive. That's the important thing. No hypothermia, which is a blessing in itself given the temperature of the water and how cold it was last night. And at least he's not alone. His father still lives here in town. John Peterson owns a construction company."

"It'll be hard for both of them."

"Yes, it will. So you see, Teresa, my reasons for asking aren't for me but for the boys. But I should be up front with you about one thing."

"What's that?"

"One of the boys I want you to talk to, Benny, is my nephew—my sister Karen's son."

The urgency of why Dennis was pushing so hard began to take shape in understanding on Teresa's face. This wasn't just a professional call. It was personal.

She nodded. "I understand."

"No, I don't think you really do. You see, Benny was the teenager who was driving one of the cars involved in the accident. Luckily, his car didn't follow Molly's into the water or last night's injuries could have been far worse than they were. We could have lost him and his friend as well. But the car did hit a tree, and now Benny's having a difficult time coping with the fact that his best friend might die from his injuries. They were pretty severe. That's the boy who was airlifted and is in a coma. It seems that he was thrown from the car. Benny won't discuss it. All he says now is that it's his fault. He's not thinking rationally. I thought it might help if you talk to him and the family."

"I doubt I'd be able to do him any good. If someone wants to blame themselves for something bad that has happened, no one can stop them."

Dennis took in the serious shadow that crossed Teresa's eyes. From what Spencer had told her, Teresa had firsthand experience with blaming herself for something that was out of her control.

He blew out an exasperated breath at the absurd way people torture themselves and how much damage it caused, which jarred her.

"I'm sorry," he said. "I've been burning the candle at both ends for the past twelve hours, and I truly feel as if I'm about to burn out completely."

"Then you need to go home and get some rest."

"Not until we finish this."

"Are you always this stubborn?"

"Look, I'm not asking you to save the world, Teresa. I'm just asking for a little help. We don't exactly have a full staff of counselors available right now. Just talk to Benny. Maybe some of the others, too. Pastor Balinski has been with Benny, but I don't think Benny is listening."

"What makes you think he'll listen to me?"

"I don't, but I'm out of options."

A gust of wind lifted Teresa's hair as a fresh group of people piled into the lodge, distracting him momentarily. She really was beautiful with her hair loose like that.

He shook his head and glanced out the floor-to-ceiling window that showed the spectacular view of the ski slopes and chairlifts leading up the mountain. It was raining lightly now. Pretty soon only the diehard skiers would stay out in the weather. Looking higher up the mountain, he saw that the clouds were dropping lower and soon it would be foggy. He needed to get back to the clinic.

Dennis pinched the bridge of his nose. The coffee cup in his hand had been drained empty, and he longed for another cup. Teresa stood and took a step toward him. For the first time since he'd arrived at the resort, she looked at him with genuine concern. No doubt his eyes looked heavy with the fatigue that was pulling at him now.

"You haven't even been to bed yet, have you?" she asked quietly.

He offered up a weak smile as his answer. How on earth could he have slept?

"Of course you haven't. People you know and love have been involved in a horrible accident. I didn't know any of them, and I had very little sleep last night myself. You look like you're about to collapse."

The waitress came over and handed Dennis a bag with his lunch. He gave her a twenty-dollar bill, and she made change for him out of her tip pouch. Teresa was right. Just the act of holding out his arm to wait for change seemed like a chore.

When the waitress was gone, Teresa said, "I don't need to tell you that you can't go on much longer without any sleep. You won't be any good to anyone in the condition you're in."

Again, it was another truth he couldn't ignore. He wasn't as young as he'd been during his residency, and the emotional toll of last night took a bigger chunk out of him than anything he'd experienced back then. "I can catch an hour or two at the clinic."

"You said you have a full house. Where will you sleep?"

"I have a cot in my office."

She grinned wryly. "That can't be too comfortable—not for a man your size."

"No," he agreed. "But I live too far out of town to take the time to drive home for a short nap and then drive back. I'll get to sleep longer if I nap at the office. In fact, I have to get back there now." He checked his watch and started to stand before she gently pushed him back in his seat.

"No, you don't." She quirked an eyebrow in challenge. "You're not going anywhere. You're exhausted."

"True enough."

"You need sleep. You and I both know you're not going to get it back at the clinic if someone is constantly coming in and interrupting you for something—which is what everyone would do, right?"

Dennis shrugged. He couldn't deny it. But why was she being so solicitous? Five minutes ago, it had seemed like she couldn't get away from him fast enough. Then it was almost as if the fight-or-flight instinct he'd triggered in her by bringing up her past had disappeared to be replaced by caring and concern.

He glanced at Teresa's determined look. Dennis had truly expected her to do an about-face and waltz up to her room as soon as he asked for help.

Especially after the conversation he'd had with Spencer.

He'd debated making that call. He knew Teresa's profession, and though he hadn't known her long, he felt he knew her well enough to be certain that turning to her for help was the right decision, even without checking her credentials. But something nagged at him about Teresa's real reason for staying so long in Stockington Falls on "vacation." She'd left Hartford a full month before Christmas—in the middle of the semester no less—and had no clear plans to return. His instincts had been confirmed by Spencer, although not with any detail. Spencer had said that she was the perfect person to help Benny but had warned that she would put up a fight. Yet here he was, a full twenty minutes after arriving, and Teresa was still sitting with him. She was even requesting that he stay. He only wished he didn't have to decline. He was needed back at the clinic.

Maybe that was one of the reasons he enjoyed being with Teresa. Like him, Teresa was driven. That much had been clear from their brief conversations. But she also had a way of making him remember with just a few words that there was more to his life than just the clinic, something that had given him tunnel vision for the months since he'd come back home to Stockington Falls.

He glanced at Teresa, at her stiff posture, her hands propped on her hips with determination. She looked at him as if she wanted nothing more than to give a stern lecture. And she looked adorable.

Her soft dark hair was hanging down this morning. Last night she'd worn it in an upswept style. He remembered the scent of her perfume drifting to him as they danced. Later, when the E.R. was full of life, remnants of her lingering perfume clinging to his shirt soothed him with the memory, reminding him that there was something more to life than just the aftermath of the horror on the bridge and the chaos right in front of him in the clinic.

Now he had Teresa's undivided attention. "I don't have to try out that cot at your office to know you'd rest better on a mattress," she said.

He arched an eyebrow. "Is that a fact?"

"Don't argue with me, Dennis. You're going to march right up to my condo and stay there for a few hours. You'll get much better rest here than if you sleep at the clinic."

"Thank you for the offer, but I can't do that, Teresa."

"I have errands to do, so it'll be quiet and you won't be disturbed. You said you have your beeper. If an emergency comes up and you're needed at the clinic, they'll call."

She was right, of course. The cot was hardly big enough for little Drew to sleep in comfortably, let alone a man his size. And everyone at the clinic knew how to get in touch with him if it was urgent. If he was there, he'd be interrupted with little things that could wait.

Still, he couldn't inconvenience her that way. He shook his head, but she pressed on.

"Who's going to take care of all those people who were hurt last night if you end up falling asleep at the wheel when *you're* driving? I'll be gone for an hour or two, and that will give you enough sleep to get through the rest of the day. It will take me at least that long to do everything I have to do, so you'll have the place to yourself. The clinic is a short drive across Abbey Bridge. It'll take you less than five minutes to get there if someone calls."

Finally, he nodded, his body shifting into low gear as if having the opportunity for sleep was all he needed to allow himself to finally shut down. He recalled the tail end of those two-day shifts when he was an intern. Somehow he'd always manage to find a second wind when needed only to collapse from exhaustion when he finally made it home.

He offered up a smile and followed her to the elevator. They walked the length of the hallway in silence. When they got to her door, she unlocked the condo and let him inside. She stayed only long enough to grab her purse and ski jacket.

"If I'm not back by the time you wake up, feel free to use the shower. There are fresh towels on the shelf."

Dennis walked past her through the narrow bedroom doorway, catching a hint of her scent. Soap. Shampoo. It smelled like fresh rain and baby powder. A much different scent than the perfume she'd been wearing last night, which was a heady fragrance of flowers and musk. He decided both seemed to fit her perfectly.

"Rest well, Dennis," she said quietly from the doorway before closing him in.

Dennis sat on the sofa and pulled off his boots. He could feel the events of the past twelve hours weighing on him, making it hard for him to move. There had been a horrible accident here in Stockington Falls, right at the base of this mountain. And he'd lost a friend. The whole town had.

Many lives now balanced dangerously on a tether, including his teenage nephew.

He hated the look on his sister's face when she'd run through the clinic door last night. The entire time he'd been stationed in Iraq, Dennis knew Karen had worried about him. It was clear from her letters. Also clear was the trouble she'd

been having with Benny. Her normally affection-
ate young son had become more distant, locking
himself in his room and only talking to her when
it was absolutely necessary. It was a common pro-
gression for some kids when they moved from boy-
hood to manhood, and he'd told her so in his letters
home. But he didn't know the extent of Benny's
withdrawal until he'd returned home from Iraq.

Dennis didn't want last night's accident to be
the straw breaking the proverbial camel's back.
He wasn't sure Benny was up to handling it, and
it was clear to him his sister was at her wits' end.
There were days he feared Karen would have a
nervous breakdown from all the stress.

He needed Teresa's help more than she knew.

Dennis got up and lazily made his way into the
bedroom. The bed was made. He'd sleep on top
and pull the throw blanket over him. As he sat on
the edge of the bed, he noticed the Bible sitting on
the nightstand. He knew the resort supplied com-
plimentary copies for its guests, but they usually
stayed tucked away in the drawer.

Warmth spread through him with the idea that
Teresa had taken the time to pull the Bible out
and place it by the bed. He fingered the pages but
kept it in its place as if left there for safekeeping.
He normally enjoyed reading a few pages of the
Bible before turning in to bed at night. It always

gave him comfort no matter what distressed him during the day. He'd kept his Bible close during his tour in Iraq.

Teresa had done the same. It was heartening and made him want to reach for the Bible himself, but he left it alone.

Instead, he stretched out and pulled the throw blanket over him, letting his mind shut down as the warmth and comfort of the bed soothed him.

Teresa hadn't agreed to help him, but she hadn't kicked him out the door either. She'd invited him in. Even after she'd discovered the circumstances of his visit. That left him an open invitation to try again.

Chapter Three

It wasn't eight hours, but the three hours of deep sleep Dennis had managed to gain were good ones. He felt rested enough that he'd be able to make it through the remainder of the day until he could go home again this evening.

He took Teresa's invitation and treated himself to a hot shower, which gave him a second wind. Wiping a clean spot in the fogged-up beveled mirror, he looked at his reflection. Without his shaving kit, he had to live with the coarse stubble of a beard on his face. He shook his head and brushed his hand over his wet hair to move the strands back into place after towel drying, and he was done.

The aroma of good food drew him through the louvered bedroom door into the suite. Teresa must have returned without him being aware of it. Now the smell of coffee was invading his senses, reminding him that he hadn't even eaten the turkey croissant before he'd fallen asleep. His stomach was growling.

"I didn't expect you to be up this soon," Teresa said as he paced over the deep pile carpet toward the kitchenette. She must have noticed the unopened sandwich and was now heating it up in the small microwave.

"I need to get back to the clinic and relieve Cammie. She has to be dead on her feet by now."

"Maybe someone has relieved her already."

"Could be, but if I know Cammie, she's still there holding down the fort even if the entire backup staff has checked in. Besides, I don't think she'd want to leave Drew and his dad just yet."

"Before you go, you'll need to eat something. Why don't you sit and drink some coffee while this sandwich finishes heating up?"

He sat down at the little dining table in the kitchenette.

"I don't want to put you out."

"You've already had the use of my digs. You might as well go all the way."

Teresa's quiet chuckle reminded him how much he enjoyed the sound of her laughter. The microwave dinged that the heating time was through. Teresa carefully took the sandwich out and placed it in front of Dennis, dropping a napkin next to the plate.

"I'm more than interested in diving into this sandwich. It smells incredible. But I'm afraid all I really have time for is coffee, Ms. Morales."

"Teresa," she said, her deep blue eyes really looking at him for the first time since he'd shown up on her doorstep over three hours ago. "You said we'd moved beyond formalities. It's time you called me Teresa. I guess you could call me Terri, but only people in my family call me Terri, except for my grandfather. He still calls me Teresa."

He'd used the formal address teasingly, but he liked that Teresa was now making a distinction of moving beyond the formal to the more personal, even telling him about the nickname.

"Is that so?" he said.

She answered quietly, as if she were a little embarrassed. "Yes."

"I happen to like Teresa. It's a pretty name. Would it bother you if I called you Teresa?"

She chuckled softly, giving her head a quick shake. "Whatever. You can really be impossible, you know that?"

"So I've been told."

"Okay. Let's cut to the chase. Why do you really want me to come to the clinic, Dennis?"

Her abrupt switch in subjects and the seriousness

of her tone had him baffled. He liked the more relaxed Teresa. But there were more pressing matters that needed attention right now.

"I think you can help Benny."

She turned for a brief moment toward the credenza and poured two cups of coffee, bringing them both to the small table where he now sat.

"It doesn't have anything to do with the conversation you had with Spencer this morning? The one where you dug up all kinds of information about my life?"

She wasn't angry. That much Dennis could tell, and he was glad she hadn't taken his snooping as a violation. He had a feeling that while he'd been chasing Zs this afternoon, she'd been seriously thinking about his request. Since she'd hit dead center on the source of his information, she'd made some calls as well.

"That was part of it," he admitted, watching her for her reaction. "But only after I'd already decided to come talk to you directly."

"Then why bother calling the superintendent of the Hartford school system on New Year's Day just to talk about a school counselor who, as far as he's concerned, is on an extended leave?"

He looked at her for a long moment and then drew in a shallow breath, letting it out slowly. "I admit that was poor judgment on my part. I've been so wrapped up in the adrenaline of last night that I wasn't thinking clearly. I'm sorry. My main concern was to get some help for my patients. For Benny."

He took a sip of coffee, hoping the caffeine would add the needed boost to his energy. Still groggy from his nap, he drank the hot liquid, careful not to burn his lips. "Besides, Spencer didn't tell me anything I didn't already know."

She laughed, but there was no humor in her tone. "You expect me to believe that?"

"He respects your privacy."

"And what about you?"

"I know something happened to make you leave Hartford. Spencer didn't have to tell me that, and he didn't tell me anything more. I've seen pain in the eyes of people before, Teresa. And I'm good at reading reactions. Even the first time you came into the clinic, when I asked you about home, your eyes grew sad. Much like they are now."

Abruptly, Teresa sat up straight in her chair and looked away. "I didn't realize I was that transparent."

"Maybe not to most people. I'm sure many might not have picked up on it, but I did. I'm right, aren't I?"

She crossed her arms over her chest in a tightly bound knot. That was body language for closing him off. She'd done it before. If they hadn't before, the warning bells certainly were going off now. She was running. That was why she'd come to Stockington Falls in the first place. She'd been running from something that had happened in Hartford. And while Dennis didn't know the details, he knew that something about this situation was bringing all those fears back, putting her on the defensive again. And a woman on the defensive wouldn't stay in town for long.

Somehow, he had to get through to her. He needed her to stay, needed her to talk to his nephew. Somehow, he knew with absolute certainty that Teresa Morales was the one who could help Benny get through this tough time he was going through. But how could he make her see that?

"Well, I have no idea what you think you see, Dennis. I don't counsel children anymore. You're looking in the wrong place. Why couldn't you have called a counselor in from St. Johnsbury?"

"I did. They want me to bring Benny up there. But his father would have nothing to do with it."

Realization shone in her eyes.

"Like I said," he continued, "I'm not looking for you to change the world. I just know that there are some kids here, my nephew included, who need some things sorted out after last night. See, I know Benny's friends. I coach them in basketball at the church community center. They're good kids. They just need direction. I think you can help give them that. And if Chuck dies…"

Teresa pulled back in the chair as if she'd been hit. Like him, Teresa worked with teenagers. She understood them better than most because she'd been entrenched in their world, knew how they reacted. If Chuck died, it wouldn't just be hard for Benny. It would be hard on his whole high school class.

Dennis reached across the table, over the empty dishes. As an invitation, he laid his hand down, palm side up, on the clean tablecloth and waited.

"I don't know," she said, looking at his out-stretched hand, then at his face. "There are too many reasons why I shouldn't."

"Give me a few, and I'll prove you wrong."

She tossed him a wry grin. "You don't have insurance for me to work at the clinic as a psychologist."

"You're not working there today. You're simply visiting some patients and talking to them off the record."

"Off the record, huh?"

He shrugged. "Insurance is not an excuse. It's a logistic. It's simply a phone call away. And permission from Benny's family isn't a problem. Karen all but begged me to have someone talk to Benny. Give me another reason."

"I'm not certified in Vermont," she said. She rolled her eyes and shook her head, already knowing he knew that wouldn't be an obstacle for very long. "Of course, you know my credentials are recognized in all fifty states and—"

"All you have to do is submit the proper paperwork here," he finished for her. "But for today, that's not a problem at all. All I want you to do is come to the clinic and talk to Benny. That's it. *I can do all things through Christ which strengtheneth me.* Do you believe that?"

He hesitated, watching her emotional turmoil change her expression. Someone who didn't genuinely care for children may not have been affected by his plea. But he knew Teresa did care, and the decision to run or stay and help was waging war with her.

"I used to."

"I really need you for this, Teresa," he said softly. "And even though I know the real reason you're not jumping in your car and heading over to the clinic with me is because something happened in Hartford and you're afraid of working with kids again, but Benny needs you."

Her face showed steep panic. Her blue eyes were filled with golden flecks of light, reflecting

her doubt and fear. Those eyes usually seemed
to glow against the darker skin that was typical
of her Latino heritage, but they just looked wide
and worried now. If he didn't know any better,
he'd think she was afraid of *him*. Or maybe it was
just the threat he posed in exposing her secret. He
hated that he'd done it. The last thing he wanted
to do was back her in a corner. But he was out of
options.

It took a moment, but the emotions that showed
on her face told him he'd been dead-on. She was
afraid. He'd seen that same fear before in his
patients, and he saw it in Benny. Taking that first
step toward healing was always the hardest. He had
the vague feeling that getting her to help him sort
out the details of last night's accident might heal
her as much as it would the people of Stockington
Falls.

After what felt like an eternity, Teresa said,
"Okay. But just for today."

Dennis ate the sandwich on the road. Teresa
followed behind him in her car as they drove to
the clinic. During the drive, she second-guessed
her decision to help a thousand times.

"Lord, I know better than to question You. But
I can't help but feel that I'm not ready for this.
What am I doing? I have no business at all going

to that clinic and talking to anyone." She said the words aloud and then immediately shrank back in her seat as if waiting for an admonishment. How could she possibly be thinking of working with another child? She'd already lost one due to her mistake. Surely God would want her to turn right around and go back to her condo and steer clear of this mess. She had no business counseling children anymore.

Teresa had assumed she and Dennis would have more time to talk before going to the clinic, if only to delay having to take that first step into Benny's room.

She had to agree with Dennis. Helping the children was more important than her fears and came first. But what if she was right and wasn't able to help Benny at all?

They drove over Abbey Bridge, and she saw up close the scars on the pavement and in the frozen ground. She thought back to the view from her window in her condo and of the many nights she had sat by that window watching in awe at the sunset over the mountain. She'd marveled how the fading light caused shadows to stretch over the covered bridge below, like a warm blanket protecting it. She loved the changing colors, the peacefulness nightfall casts against the bridge and on Stockington Falls Mountain. It gave her a safe place to explore all the thoughts that haunted her.

But now everywhere she looked where she'd once seen beauty the remains of disaster seemed to glare up at her mockingly. It made her mind return to darker memories, like the day she'd first driven into Stockington Falls. She'd still had on the dress she'd worn to Mariah's funeral.

That was the day she'd haphazardly packed her bags with whatever she could get her hands on. She'd gotten into her car and driven north. She didn't have a clue as to where she was going. All she cared about when she'd left Hartford was getting away. Her journey had brought her to Stockington Falls.

She hadn't planned on staying here more than a week, maybe two. Just enough time to sort her own thoughts out in her head. Circumstance had her staying a little longer—and making the acquaintance of a certain doctor.

She'd liked Dennis right from the first time they'd met but would have liked it if their first meeting hadn't been because she'd twisted her ankle on the first day she'd put skis on. With a bruised ankle and a bruised ego, she'd hobbled into the clinic and had gotten a stern lecture from Dennis about not stepping foot on a pair of skis until her injury had completely healed. Despite her embarrassment at being scolded, the doctor's genuine concern and charming smile had had her feeling just like any one of the lovesick schoolgirls she counseled who sported their mammoth crushes on the star basketball players.

After hurting her ankle, she'd called the school to talk about taking more time off and learned about a friend's need to sublet an apartment for a few months until her new house was ready to be moved into. Impulsively, Teresa had offered up her Hartford condo, which meant she wouldn't be going home for a few months.

That was a month ago, and she'd come no closer to getting herself ready to return to her home, her job and her place at the Hartford school where she'd worked for years. The excuse she'd given the principal was that she had to stay and follow up with the local doctor. Even now as she thought about it, it had been a feeble excuse, one that masked her real reason for being so willing to leave everything behind in the first place. She was still terrified. She remembered how as she sat in church during the funeral services she'd felt as though every eye was on her, blaming her for not stepping in sooner. For not doing something to prevent an already difficult tragedy from becoming worse.

Dennis was right on another point. She *was* transparent. The only person she was fooling by using the excuse of needing local medical treatment was herself! She could have easily gone home to be seen by her own doctor in Hartford.

And she could have just gone home and dealt with what had happened instead of subletting her condo. End of story.

But that would have meant facing painful realizations she wasn't yet ready to face. That scared her more than anything Dennis Harrington could throw at her.

Now finances were low, and she'd have to do a little creative juggling to keep herself afloat for a while. But she had some time. She'd get the newspaper on the way back to the resort and spend the evening looking through the classifieds for an inexpensive apartment to rent. If not here in Stockington Falls then it would be somewhere else. It wouldn't be as luxurious as the resort, but it would do.

Finding an apartment seemed so *permanent* when in truth she really didn't know how much longer she wanted to stay in Vermont.

You're running again, Teresa, she thought to herself.

The teacher who had been subletting her condo had it until the beginning of March. That seemed like such a long way away, and Teresa hadn't thought much beyond that.

She pulled into the parking lot of the clinic and parked next to Dennis's SUV. After killing the engine and securing her vehicle, Teresa got out of the car as a wave of panic hit her square in the chest.

What am I doing here? How am I ever going to get through this?

One foot in front of the other, Teresa strode through the tinted glass clinic doors beside Dennis.

As she and Dennis walked into the open reception area, Teresa was immediately struck by the odd sense of movement that surrounded her. When she'd visited the clinic almost a month ago, it had been quiet, the rooms virtually empty. She'd been the only one in the waiting room, which at the time had seemed peculiar to her. You couldn't stop at any of the clinics in Hartford without expecting to wait at least an hour before being seen by a doctor. Today, the waiting room was still quiet, but it was clear from the sound of monitors and the writing on the white board by the nurses' station that rooms that had once been empty were now occupied with patients.

"I didn't expect you back so soon," a woman from behind the reception desk said, her gaze lifting from a clipboard. Her eyes were red-rimmed and droopy, her shoulders bent with a weight so great Teresa felt herself sag beneath it just looking at her.

"I should have known you wouldn't go home," Dennis said.

"You worry too much," the woman said softly, sweeping her gaze to Teresa and then back at Dennis.

Teresa remembered seeing her here the day she'd twisted her ankle and guessed that this was Cammie Reynolds, the nurse Dennis had mentioned back at the lodge.

Cammie sighed. "John's in with Drew. He wants to take him home tonight. Now that things have calmed down, I figured I'd go with them just to make sure they're both okay. Drew might sleep a little better if he's in his own bed."

"You're right," Dennis said warmly. "I'll sign his release and have John bring him back tomorrow to have the permanent cast put on."

"Benny is still here. Your sister is worried about taking him home." Cammie shot another glance at Teresa void of emotion. "Did you bring her here to talk to Benny?"

"Yes. Any incidents we should know about?"

Cammie shook her head, her shoulder-length amber hair drifting back and forth over her slender shoulders with the movement. "He's not saying anything more than what he's already told us."

Teresa noticed the glance that passed between Cammie and Dennis. Just how resistant had Benny been to talking about the accident?

Without another word, she turned and followed Dennis down the narrow corridor toward one of the medical center rooms.

"Hey, Benny," Dennis said as he walked into the room at the end of the hall. "How are you feeling this morning?"

The boy turned a stone face toward the window. He didn't utter so much as a groan in response to his uncle.

Dennis smiled warmly at the woman who was sitting next to Benny's bed, clearly Dennis's sister. Teresa could see the resemblance, though she looked older than Dennis by several years. But worrying over a child would do that to a person.

Gray streaks sliced through her black hair, which was pulled back in a tight ponytail. She wore an oversize ski sweater over baggy denim jeans, both wear-worn with age. By the black circles under her eyes and hunch in her posture, Teresa guessed she'd been seated by her son's side since the moment he'd arrived at the hospital.

Dennis made quick introductions and then said, "Karen, would you give us a few minutes, please?"

Karen nodded silently, giving Dennis's arm a

squeeze, and then walked to the door, reluctantly closing it behind her.

Teresa took a good look at her new patient. Benny hadn't grown up in the tough streets of the city. Stockington Falls wasn't even a dot on the map save the ski resort that made it known outside the state. But the stubborn set of his jaw and long hair dyed jet-black would make him fit in among the kids she knew in Hartford. If Teresa dug deep and looked at the clothes Benny had been wearing last night during the accident, she was sure she'd find a well-worn pair of baggy jeans and snowboard or basketball T-shirt among his things.

He'd been spared the acne that so many kids suffered with at seventeen, but he did have small bald patches where his light beard was still downy and hadn't fully matured. He probably only bothered to shave at all but once or twice a week, most likely at his mother's urging. "I hear you're itching to get out of here, Benny," Dennis said.

Still no response from the boy.

Dennis checked the chart at the end of the bed. "Everything looks pretty good. How does that shoulder feel?"

Silence.

He gave a quick glance to Teresa and then back to Benny. She'd known Dennis only a short time, but the love and concern she saw in those deep eyes was unmistakable. He was afraid for his nephew. And that did nothing to dispel the skitter of nerves crawling through her veins.

"I'd like you to meet a friend of mine, Benny. Her name is Teresa Morales."

Benny didn't acknowledge her at all, so Teresa gave it a try. "Your uncle told me you're quite the basketball player."

When Benny still showed no movement, Teresa touched Dennis by the arm. "If I could have a moment or two. It might be easier if we're alone."

Dennis nodded and then sighed much like Karen had. There was no guarantee that Benny would talk to a stranger any more than he would talk to his own family, but at least she had experience with dealing with teenagers and the silence.

"I'll be in Allie Pryor's room or in my office if you need me," Dennis said. It may have been her imagination, but he seemed to hesitate for a fraction of a moment, as if he wanted to tell her something.

She ignored the warning bells that clanged in her head. Dennis had simply asked her to come talk to the kid. It was the morning after something horrific had happened, and surely Benny had conflicting feelings about his part in all of it.

When the door closed behind Dennis, Teresa

forced her thoughts back to Benny's room and took a deep breath to steel herself for what was to come. Unfortunately, she'd been through this very scenario more times than she wanted to count. Guilt, betrayal, blame, grief. All that had to be sorted out in one's mind before healing could occur.

She turned, taking a stride into the room, and sat down next to the teenager. She had her work cut out for her.

"I'm sure you know why I came here today, Benny." No answer. She tried a different tactic. "But let's put all that aside and just talk for a bit, get to know each other."

He turned his head toward her, his face void of emotion. She could almost feel the anger inside him simmering just below the surface of his composure. "Why?"

"You look like a pretty nice guy. Why not?"

He turned and looked toward the window again. She stifled a sigh.

"Why don't we talk about sports? Your uncle said you're an athlete. I'm not much into basketball. I'm a hockey fan myself. What about you?"

The slight movement of his shoulder could hardly be deemed a shrug, but Teresa would take whatever she could get at this point.

"I'm a big Bruins fan. My dad used to take me to the games when I was little. I don't have much time for it now, but I manage to see a game every now and then."

That earned her a roll of the eyes from Benny. Good. Progress.

She chuckled quietly. "Okay, so you don't like the Bruins. Or is it hockey you're not fond of?"

"Hockey's okay if you're into getting your face bashed on the ice. It doesn't take much to skate around and swing a stick."

"Fair enough. So basketball is more your thing?"

No comment.

"Are you on the team at school?"

"You already said Uncle Dennis told you I play basketball."

"He said you were on the team at the community center. I was just wondering if you were playing on the high school team. You know a lot of kids get college scholarships when they're good enough at athletics."

Benny stiffened. "Won't matter if I do."

"What do you mean?"

"I'm...not going to college."

"Why not? If you want to go, an athletic or academic scholarship is one of the best ways to make it happen."

"Because I probably won't live long enough to make it out of high school."

It took everything Teresa had not to shrink back in her seat. Fighting for air, she tried to find the right words to respond. Was he worried about his injuries? Dennis surely assured Benny that his injuries weren't that severe and he'd make a full recovery.

Fearful of what might come, Teresa proceeded slowly. "Benny, what makes you think you won't live long enough to make it to graduation?"

Benny regarded her seriously. "The accident didn't manage to kill me, so I guess I'll have to do it myself."

It was just under a half hour since Dennis had left Teresa with Benny when he saw her barreling down the hallway, wildly forcing her arms through her jacket sleeves. He'd convinced Karen to run across the street for a bite to eat. Louise, the day waitress at the Twin Falls Café, was good at bending an ear, and his sister would surely need that now.

All seemed normal again, until Teresa came charging toward him. He stepped into her path before she could advance any farther.

"Move, Dennis," she ground out, barely looking at him.

"Whoa. Hold on." He caught her by the upper arms. She quickly thrashed his hands off her. It was a good thing the clinic had cleared out and was now pleasantly quiet. He had the nagging feeling this scene was going to get ugly.

"Get out of my way."

"What happened in there? What's wrong with you?"

"With me? What about him?" Although they were virtually alone, her voice had lowered considerably as she pointed back toward the room she'd just fled. Benny's room.

"He's still in shock. It was a horrible accident," he said, stating the obvious.

"Spencer *did* tell you, didn't he? He told you what happened at the school."

She stalked past him, the heels of her boots echoing down the empty hall as she charged.

"I told you I talked with him this morning, but he said nothing about why you left Hartford. He only assured me that I'd be in good hands with you helping here at the clinic. And I already knew that," he said, catching up with her and falling into her step.

As she reached the door to the clinic, he gripped her arm and swung her around. His breath lodged in his throat when he saw her eyes brimming with unshed tears. She was visibly shaking.

"What happened in there?" he demanded.

She glanced around and saw that they were

alone. "You didn't tell me Benny has a history of being suicidal, Dennis. That he's tried to kill himself twice already."

He sighed, regret eating away at his insides. Yes, he should have told her. He thought he'd have more time in the room with Teresa and Benny so that it all could be brought out in the open.

"I should have told you," he agreed wearily.

"It was important. I never would have come here if I'd known."

Pushing through the door, she stepped out into the darkness. He followed her. The bitter cold bit through his thin hospital jacket, assaulting his skin.

"He needs you, Teresa."

As she swung around, she swiped at her face. Her movements were quick and thrashing, her arms swinging as she paced back and forth. It was more than evident her reaction was not just about Benny. There was something more. Spencer had implied as much, telling him he thought Teresa might need someone like Benny, too.

"She won't think she can help," Spencer had said on the phone. "In fact, I'm sure she'll flat-out refuse. But you talk her into it. Whatever you do, make her do it."

At the time, Dennis was already too tired and too worried about what his nephew might do to think what that meant. Now that one statement and its true meaning nagged at him.

Teresa stopped pacing for a moment. "He needs help. I'll give you that. But it can't be from me, Dennis. I can't do it. He needs something more than what I can give him."

"Maybe so. But right now you're all he has."

She shook her head. "I'm sure there are plenty of facilities within an hour's drive of here with doctors who can help him. Really help him."

"That's just it. He'll never get to one."

"Why not?"

"Not everyone thinks therapy is a good thing. There are a lot of folks around here who'd see it as a weakness."

Her shoulders slumped. "Admitting you need help isn't being weak."

"I know that, and you know that. I'll even venture to guess my sister will agree to that, too. Unfortunately, my brother-in-law Frank is of the breed that thinks secrets are better left locked in a closet. He's fought all attempts to have Benny placed in therapy, despite my recommendation and that of his physician after the first two attempts on his life. He thinks Benny is just doing this to get attention because he's a little depressed."

"But one day he may actually succeed," Teresa said.

"That's what I'm trying to prevent. Frank has even refused to have Pastor Balinski counsel Benny. It's become a tug of war in the house. After last night's accident, Karen is now without a car, so the chances of Benny's dad taking him to therapy on his own are slim to none."

The car was the least of their problems. Dennis would drive Benny to St. Johnsbury himself if it wasn't going to cause an escalation in the kind of friction between his sister and her husband that he'd seen since he'd come home from Iraq.

"It's not uncommon for teenagers to become depressed," Dennis said. "I know that. But something has gotten under Benny's skin. I don't know what it is, and he's not talking about it—at least not to anyone who wants to help him. I don't know if tension in the house is causing Benny to act out or if the tension is a result of Benny's behavior. But I know that I need you, Teresa. He needs you."

Things had changed in his family when Dennis was away. The family that seemed to have it all now appeared to be crumbling right before his eyes, and he felt powerless to stop it.

When Teresa lifted her chin, something had changed in her expression. She was closed off just like she had been when he first made his request this afternoon.

"I'm sorry, Dennis, but I just can't help you here. I'll only make things worse."

Turning on her heels, she escaped into the cold darkness. Dennis didn't bother to go after her. He could tell she needed some time to herself. There was definitely something more than just poor Benny and his problems on her mind. Something was eating at her—maybe whatever was haunting her that had brought her to Stockington Falls.

He turned and strode back through the clinic doors, making a silent prayer to the Lord to find the answers. For all their sakes.

Chapter Four

Teresa had let it go way too long, she thought, looking at the bottom line of her check register. In an effort to forget the catastrophic episode at the clinic, Teresa had spent the night toying with her finances, and now knew she was in even bigger trouble financially than she had thought.

Dennis had been right about another thing. Hartford's school system, while generous in pay, didn't afford her the comfort to live in the lap of luxury for too long.

She tossed the checkbook back into her purse and pushed the classified ad she'd pulled from the morning newspaper aside. She held the warm ceramic mug of coffee between both hands and glanced out the window of the Twin Falls Café. Across the street was the Stockington Falls Medical Clinic. She'd fled the clinic the other day like a child spooked at a horror film.

Ridiculous. She was a professional, after all, and that day she'd been anything but. She couldn't blame Dennis if he were angry. She was angry— at herself and at the situation. At whoever was responsible for that accident, forcing her into res- urrecting all the past ugliness she fought to leave behind in Hartford.

Lord, what if I fail again? What if I miss some important sign? I can't let down Benny that way. Not like I did with Mariah.

More than anything, Teresa feared that if she wasn't able to reach him through counseling, it was Benny who'd suffer the most, not just from his own fears and self-blame, but from the thought that he was beyond being helped. He'd view her weakness as his fault.

Walking into Benny's room, she'd thought she was in control. But as Benny just stared at her, instead of spewing typical adolescent vulgarities to vent, as she'd expected, she saw Mariah's haunting eyes staring back at her. Teresa tried to remember the carefree smile she'd seen so many times before or that laughter that had always filtered into her office at the school before Mariah came bouncing in. But that was gone. She hadn't been able to bring any of that joy back.

All she saw was Mariah's limp body lying on her childhood bed. It was as if the image was permanently fixed in her mind. She only hoped that memory, that image, would be something that with God's grace she would eventually be able to erase from her mind.

Mariah had been just seventeen, like Benny. But unlike Benny, Mariah succeeded in taking her life as well as that of her unborn child.

A cold chill raced up Teresa's spine and made her shudder. She quickly took a large gulp of her coffee, but it did nothing to dissipate the feeling.

Mariah had never told Teresa about the baby. If she had, maybe Teresa would have seen the signs of desperation. She would have paid more attention. Some kids were good at hiding, laughing on the outside, while inside the pain ate away at them. It had to for her to have been driven to the point of wanting to give up.

Now Teresa questioned the real truth of what had led up to that day. Mariah had spoken about her boyfriend David, and she had seen the pair entwined in the halls, in front of their lockers and in the corner of the building during lunch. They'd seemed so happy. David and Mariah had genuinely seemed in love, which was why she knew that Mariah had been devastated when David was killed in a car accident the week before the last time Mariah came to talk to her.

But Mariah hadn't come to her because of

David's death or about the baby she was carrying. She wanted to talk about "her friend" and the problems her friend was having with other students. And Teresa hadn't seen that Mariah's "friend" was really Mariah until it was too late.

Teresa had met with a lot of students at the high school who didn't want to acknowledge the horrible truths of the trauma inflicted on them by bullying. It was easier to pretend it was happening to someone else.

Yes, Teresa had failed Mariah by not seeing the signs of bullying that led to her suicide. That one mistake would haunt her for the rest of her life.

"Ms. Morales?"

Teresa pulled herself out of the past to look up at the woman standing in front of her.

"Yes," she said. "I'm Teresa Morales."

The woman smiled. "I don't mean to interrupt your breakfast—"

"No, not at all." She recognized the woman but didn't immediately place the face.

"Karen Dulton? Dennis Harrington's sister. We met yesterday at the clinic when you talked to my son, Benny." Karen reached out a hand to shake Teresa's.

"Oh, yes, please sit down."

Karen shook her head. "I can't stay. I'm on my way out to do errands while I still have the car."

The shame over not immediately recognizing Dennis's sister mixed in with what had happened yesterday at the clinic made Teresa want to crawl into a hole. "I'm sorry. My mind was elsewhere. How is Benny doing today?"

"The same, physically. But his injuries will heal."

"And his friend, Chuck? Do you have an update on him?"

Karen's expression clouded. "Still in a coma. Still in critical condition. I try not to talk about it with Benny. It only upsets him."

"I understand."

Silence hung heavy between the two women for a brief moment. Karen must have something she wanted to say—she had clearly sought Teresa out. If she'd only stopped into the café for a quick drink or bagel, she could easily have left without saying hello. It was Karen who broke the silence.

"I was hoping you'd reconsider seeing Benny again. I know how difficult he can be sometimes."

"No, no. He wasn't difficult with me yesterday." The last thing Teresa wanted was for Karen to misunderstand her reaction to Benny yesterday. "He must be so confused right now."

Karen quickly sat, propping her purse in her lap. "He is. And truth be known, I'm really afraid for him. I was even before the accident, but now it's worse. I feel like I'm losing him sometimes. Do you know what I mean?"

Tears welled up in Karen's eyes, knowing the notion of losing a child was unbearable to a parent.

"Yes, I do know what you mean. I've worked with teenagers for over ten years. They can be very difficult until they find their way—and even when they do."

"Pastor Balinski said as much. But Benny doesn't want to talk to the pastor of our church. He doesn't really want to talk to anyone. Not even me. Especially not me."

Karen was hurting. That much was evident. "I'm not sure how long I'm going to be in Stockington Falls," Teresa hedged. "I don't know how much help I can be."

Karen gave it one more try. "Maybe if you talk to Benny again? I'd really appreciate it. If I can get him to a point where he's open to seeing someone on a regular basis… I'm just asking."

No, Karen wasn't asking. She was pleading. And Teresa couldn't help but sympathize with her.

"I can't make any promises, but I'll think about it."

A smile split Karen's face, and in that instant, Teresa could see the family resemblance between

Dennis and his sister. "That's all I'm asking. Thank you."

As Karen walked away, Teresa thought about yesterday's disaster. But today was another day. A child needed her help. She had to put her own failures behind her at least enough to be of some use to someone. Maybe Benny. Maybe not.

"Sorry I'm late."

Teresa blinked hard and pulled herself from yesterday's events back to the café as Vanessa Kaufmann slid her impeccably dressed body onto the bench on the opposite side of the booth.

"You know, we could have met for coffee in your condo or at the lodge," she said, peeling her coral mohair wrap from her head, revealing platinum hair only a hairdresser could love. Despite the glowing hair, the woman was stunning, Teresa thought without any envy. It wasn't that Vanessa was particularly beautiful. Without the glitter and pamperings to keep her nearly fifty-year-old face from looking her true age, no one would pick her out in a crowd.

But Vanessa Kaufmann *was* stunning. She knew how to dress herself up, and she knew how to work a room of people so that if they didn't notice her when she first walked in, they knew who she was mere moments after her arrival.

In a way, Teresa envied her for that but not like

many other women would. It was the surety in which Vanessa moved through life that Teresa found intriguing. She wondered if the fifteen years that spanned between them would enable her to possess that same confidence. Right now, Teresa wondered if Vanessa had ever had a moment's doubt in her life.

"If you want to hang out with me, you're going to have to develop an appetite for simple foods instead of all the rich stuff that chef of yours serves at every meal. I swear I gain five pounds just looking at the menu." As the co-owner of the ski resort along with her husband, Vanessa usually suggested that they eat at the lodge's restaurant, but Teresa had called a stop to that. She was on a budget now—and a diet.

Vanessa laughed in a way that turned heads in the small café. It drew attention but didn't annoy any of the tourists happily eating their steak and eggs.

"Jacques and I have an understanding. Rich is only good if it keeps me neatly tucked into my ski pants. He would have made a simple spread for us and sent it up to your condo personally. You'd like Jacques. He's a doll." She laughed again and then gave Teresa a knowing grin. "But then, you've got your eye on Dr. Harrington, don't you?"

"How would you know?"

"I saw you with him New Year's Eve. You looked like quite the item if you ask me. And I loved every minute of it, too. For the past month you've been hanging out at the lodge with all these incredibly hunky guys on the ski slope and you don't even look at them. It's about time someone caught your eye. And I'm happy for Dennis, too. He needs to see more than the walls of that clinic."

"We were just dancing and talking."

"It wasn't the dancing that was a dead giveaway, honey. It was the way you were looking at each other."

"Is that so?"

"I wasn't the only one who noticed."

"Well, I won't be staying much longer," Teresa said just as the waitress dropped a mug of coffee on the table in front of Vanessa. She silently motioned to the waitress to warm her cup as well.

When the waitress left, Vanessa leaned forward, a concerned glint in her eye. "What do you mean? Did you and Dennis have a fight that I didn't see? I noticed he didn't stay till the end of the party."

"You must live in a bubble, Van. Dennis was called away because of the accident."

Vanessa slouched back against the booth. "That's right. Amazing, huh? One of the biggest nights around here for ages and then something like this happens. But I don't believe for one minute that

Dennis leaving the party early is what's driving you away."

What could she say? She hadn't known Vanessa for more than a month, even though she'd been one of the first people Teresa had met in town. Since then they'd struck up an immediate friendship that Teresa had come to enjoy.

"I'm either going to have to start waiting tables at the lodge or lower my standard of luxury."

"Money." Vanessa practically spat out the word. "It's at the root of all heartache, I tell you. It's all Hal can talk about. It's not as if there isn't a fortune on that mountain over there, but each year he's always worried the tourists won't come. They always do."

She poured some cream in her coffee and then leaned forward. "Don't worry about your bill. I can take care of it."

Teresa gasped. "You will not. I won't take advantage of our friendship that way."

Vanessa eyed Teresa wickedly. "Being the co-owner should have some perks. Beside, Hal charges too much for those condos anyway. So, are you going back over to the clinic later to make up with Dennis after you stormed out of there yesterday?"

Teresa's mouth dropped open. "How did you know about that?"

With a shrug, Vanessa said, "You don't keep secrets in Stockington Falls like you do in Hartford, dear Teresa. People talk. A lot. I should know. There's been plenty said both to my face and behind my back about Hal and the way he looks at other women."

"I'm sorry."

Vanessa waved her off. "Don't be. I came to terms with my husband years ago. He loves me. Look but don't touch—that's what I say."

Teresa couldn't imagine being in a marriage where love and respect weren't at the core. Vanessa was too confident a woman not to be hurt by what her husband was doing, especially when there was talk around town. But she respected her friend's feelings enough to let the topic drop.

"So?" Vanessa pressed.

Glancing at the steam rising from her coffee mug, Teresa said, "I haven't decided yet."

It surprised even her that she'd gone from flat-out refusal to return to the clinic to indecision in the span of twenty-four hours. But it was true. She wasn't sure she could face Benny again. But something inside her questioned if fleeing from Benny and the challenge he represented—like a child hiding from her punishment—was the way she wanted to keep things. She'd been a coward. And that didn't sit well with her.

"That poor boy," Vanessa was saying, somewhere in the distance, as Teresa thought back on Benny's face…and Mariah's, and Mariah and David. "Now he's without a mother."

She snapped her gaze back to Vanessa, and for the first time, she realized she was talking about Drew, not Benny.

"Ah, I know," Teresa said, dragging in a deep breath.

"They say he was spared from the explosion, then somehow managed to escape the car and get to the river bank. I'm sure his father is thanking the Lord right now for his blessing. To lose a wife and a child… God was with little Drew for sure."

Teresa hadn't read the papers yesterday. And she was sure there were lingering articles in today's edition, but she'd avoided reading those as well. She'd seen enough the night of the accident.

The poor child. Teresa could only imagine what he'd seen, what he was experiencing now with the loss of his mother. Between Drew and Benny, no wonder Dennis was so insistent that she come to the clinic.

Teresa made a mental note to ask Dennis about little Drew. In that instant, she suddenly decided to stop fleeing like a child and look in on one or two of them instead.

* * *

"Am I being too presumptuous in saying I knew you'd be back?"

Teresa stared up at Dennis's face. It wasn't smug. That really wasn't his style. He was just too handsome with the little lines that creased his eyes when he smiled and the way he cocked his head to one side just so when he was looking at her.

Memories of New Year's Eve crashed around her. She liked Dennis, more than she suspected she should if she had half a brain. He was a good man. The fact that she was still single at thirty-five was because she'd come to the conclusion there was a shortage of good men in the world. And here she was looking at one of them.

But the thought of anything remotely resembling a relationship right now made her heart go into a panic.

Teresa crossed her arms. "Let me guess. Your sister called you?"

"About twenty minutes ago. Karen asked if I could give her a ride just in case she couldn't get the family truck."

She nodded. "I thought it'd be a good idea to check in on Drew and Benny."

"I'm glad."

Teresa had learned from Louise, the waitress at the Twin Falls Café, that Benny had been released yesterday afternoon after she'd met with him and that Karen Dulton had pleaded with her stubborn husband, Frank, to take Benny to St. Johnsbury for some help. But the answer was still no. Why any parent would refuse help for their child, especially when that child was so desperately in need, was beyond Teresa's comprehension.

That was when Teresa made the decision to call Benny's mother herself and let her know she would be at the clinic if Benny was open to coming in. Karen had jumped at the opportunity to have Teresa meet with Benny again.

Now that she was standing in front of Dennis, the weight of unfinished business crashed in around her. "Can we talk a minute before Benny and Karen get here?"

Dropping a clipboard into place, Dennis turned to face her. "Things are quiet here. We can talk more privately in my office, though."

The smell of the clinic was a familiar one. Teresa followed Dennis through the reception area along the corridor she'd raced down yesterday toward a set of offices in the back. Dennis's name was on his office door.

He dropped down on the small sofa instead of in the seat behind the worn-looking metal desk. Teresa noted that while most of the clinic looked clean and new, Dennis had clearly placed new office furniture low on his list of priorities.

"I expected you to be long gone from Stockington Falls after what happened yesterday. But when Karen called..."

Teresa shook her head. "What happened...that was wrong of me. There were a thousand different ways I could have handled that situation, and I chose the absolute wrong one. I apologize for that."

"What makes you think you aren't human?"

She feigned shock. "You mean I am?"

"Oh, yes, ma'am. You most definitely are a creature of the human race. You're allowed to make a mistake or two."

She cleared her throat. She wasn't ready for this easy banter. She'd been fully prepared to just be professional again.

Gratitude filled her heart. "You're too kind, Dennis. You let me off the hook much too easily."

"It's not easy dealing with teenagers. Especially Benny. So it's no trouble to cut you a little slack. You're going to need it."

She chuckled. "I wanted to clear things up about Benny and to talk about how things will be handled with him and anyone else I work with."

Dennis leaned forward and pulled a paper from

the top of his desk. "I spoke with the insurance company and added you. It's not uncommon for medical staff to do per diem work in small towns, and you can do that while you're here in Stockington Falls. Work as much or as little as you want and be paid through the clinic. I know you're on vacation but—"

"No, that's perfect. I don't want a full schedule. I'll just come in a few days a week if that's good."

"Perfect."

"I told your sister that it was better to meet someplace neutral rather than at her house where Frank might interfere and Benny might feel intimidated."

"I agree. Karen was worried about that. There must be some space at the resort—"

"That won't be an option. I won't be there much longer."

"You could meet at the church community center. Benny's comfortable there. He's on the basketball team that Fred Ducombe and I coach. I don't think Pastor Balinski would mind giving you the use of one of the rooms for a private session."

"His friends will be around. I'm not sure he'll open up to me if he's afraid his peers will know he's seeing a psychologist. Even if you tell them I'm just a friend, kids have a way of digging up information. They might rib him about it and then I will have lost him, especially in light of how his father feels about him seeing me."

Dennis nodded in agreement.

"Besides, a neutral location would give him a place to truly be himself, without worrying about other people around, expecting him to behave a certain way. Benny seems so confused about a lot of things. He feels guilty and is punishing himself."

"That's not uncommon after an accident."

"No. But the root of his problems started long before the accident."

"True."

"I'm afraid that having the pastor close by may prevent him from opening up, too. Is he close to Pastor Balinski? Do you think talking with him will help?"

"I'm not sure. Karen has always had a strong faith in God, and I know she's done her best to instill those beliefs in Benny."

"Then it's best to be somewhere where there are no outside influences. I was hoping I could meet with Benny here. If that's okay with you and there is room, of course."

"It's fine," he said quickly. "In fact, it's great. I would have offered the clinic initially, but I wasn't sure how you'd feel about it after yesterday. I don't want *you* to feel intimidated, either. I pushed you pretty hard to come here."

She shook her head. "It wasn't you, Dennis. It was me. I overreacted. It's not going to be a problem again. And I think here is actually the best place for Benny to come. Since you're his uncle, his friends won't necessarily question why he's here, and it'll be easier to get him transportation to and from sessions."

"He also won't feel like all eyes are on him."

"Exactly."

"Good. We can convert the spare room into an office so you can meet with Benny and Drew, if John's agreeable to bringing him in."

"There may not be any signs of problems with Drew for a while. Kids deal with death different than adults, especially at that age. But I'll talk to John and let him know what he can expect from Drew in the coming months."

"I know I only asked you to talk to the boys, but there may be a few other people in town, especially the kids in Benny's class, who may feel like talking."

She raised an eyebrow.

"I know," Dennis replied. "That'll be a bigger challenge and definitely not what you signed on for."

"Weren't you the one who said you weren't

expecting me to heal the world? I did say per diem."

"Yes. But can you blame a guy for trying? And since you're here… Anyway, the office is just filled with some boxes now. But we can move them into the storage area. You decide how much of a load you want to take on."

"Fair enough."

"Teresa," he said, pausing. "I'm really glad you're here for my nephew."

She didn't answer, and Dennis quickly changed the subject. "So what's this about you leaving your condo?"

Teresa cleared her throat. "I won't be staying at the resort anymore, or I won't be as soon as I can find another place. You were right about one thing. The school system pays well but not nearly enough to keep me in such luxurious accommodations as the condo I have at the resort. As much as I like it there, I'll end up draining my retirement fund if I stay much longer. As it is, I'd only planned on staying a few weeks, and I've already gone past that plan."

"Well, we can't have you going broke. So you're looking for a house to rent?"

"I don't know that I need a whole house. Maybe a small apartment that's furnished. There must be something like that around here. It's just me, and

I don't have much with me so it won't need to be fancy."

"I have room at my place," he said quickly and without reservation.

She glanced at his face and saw that Dennis was serious. That much she had learned to recognize. This wasn't the flirtatious Dennis who she'd met around town in the past month who was easy to banter with. This was the professional, no-nonsense man who bandaged her foot without any emotion and told her in no uncertain terms to stay off a pair of skis until her foot healed.

"I don't think that's a good idea. I'm not really looking to rent a room in someone's home."

He shook his head slightly. "Not in my house. I have a small guest cottage behind the house. It's not much, but the rent is cheap—free—and it has all the essentials. Most importantly, you'll have your own space and privacy."

"You aren't renting it out?"

"I'd planned to, but I've just been too busy to even think of it this winter. Besides, the only thing available this time of the year in Stockington Falls is ski rentals, and you'll pay an arm and a leg for a weekly rental unless you sign a full year's lease."

"Really? I didn't realize renting a place would be that expensive."

"This is our busy season. Housing is in high

demand. It'll be cheaper in the summer, but that won't help you now. You won't be able to find a better deal than what I'm offering. Between my work at the clinic and with the church community center, I'm hardly ever at home. When I'm not there you'll have all the privacy you want, and you won't be locked into signing a lease."

Dennis leaned back against the love seat and shook his head slightly. "Benny is almost eighteen years old. He'll be graduating in a few months. I want to make sure he makes it long enough to wear that cap and gown. Besides, you'll be comfortable at the guesthouse. It's quiet, almost too much so for me sometimes," he said, a sadness deepening his voice.

Biting her bottom lip, she said, "I don't know."

His dark eyes seemed to bore into her, and she had to remember that his offer was simply a way for him to show his gratitude. After all, Benny was his sister's son. If she was able to make ends meet by staying in a guesthouse for free, she could stay longer and make sure Benny was okay before she went home. The offer didn't have any strings attached and didn't need to be complicated by her attraction to Dennis.

"It could be a good solution. That is, if you're really sure," she said.

"I'm sure. And if you end up hating it there, you

can always explore some other possibility. But at least this way you have an affordable option."

An affordable housing option was important. But there were other things Teresa wanted to explore, too, such as Dennis and the way he made her feel. She'd worked with men in the past. It had never been a problem. In fact, Teresa found that a good working relationship many times meant gaining a friend like she had in working with Spencer. But this was different. Teresa could already see Dennis affected her in a way she hadn't felt with any of her other colleagues, even when he was being practical and professional.

There was something warm and safe about Dennis. It wasn't just that she enjoyed his company. Something about him settled her to the core, grounding her. He seemed so solid, and in her life there had been men who were anything but.

Her mother's three marriages during the span of Teresa's youth had made her believe that lasting love was something that only existed in fairy tales. The men Teresa had known had always been nice, treated her well and then something would end it. Teresa knew that the problems usually stemmed from her reluctance to let someone in. During college, it was easier to push herself into her studies than to give any of the men she'd met there serious attention. As an adult, it was work and the kids that drove Teresa. She couldn't exactly blame any of the men she'd known for leaving when she'd given them every indication that her heart wasn't in the relationship.

And now there was Dennis. Did she really want to be in such close contact with a man who seemed to occupy her thoughts so frequently?

"Thank you."

"After you're finished with Benny, I'll take you out to the house and show you around," he said. "I don't have anything else on my schedule today other than paperwork."

As she walked out of Dennis's office, a wave of panic hit her square in her chest, choking the air out of her. Was she really ready to meet Benny again? And what about this move to the cottage at Dennis's place?

Both moves seemed too close for comfort. Yet Teresa knew she couldn't continue to run from everything that sent her heart into a panic.

The only thing Teresa knew for sure was that she'd been running for a long time. Right now her feet were pointed in a direction that scared her. But her feet were still moving forward. That had to be a good thing.

Chapter Five

"Don't look at me that way, Dennis," Karen said. His sister was standing in the doorway of his office, her arms crossed in front of her. Benny was still in his session with Teresa, and he was sure the wait was eating at Karen.

"What way?"

"I know you too well. You've got something to say, and you don't know how to say it."

"Come in and have a seat."

Karen's face registered steep panic as she quickly sat in the seat opposite his desk. "What is it? Is there something wrong with Benny? I thought you said he was going to be fine."

He dispelled her panic with the wave of his hand. "No, Benny's a strong kid. He's going to be fine, physically."

Realization dawned in her eyes. "You mean emotionally. But isn't that why he's meeting with Teresa, so she can help?"

He nodded. Dennis couldn't deny that he'd been preoccupied with Benny and what his sister had termed the boy's *distance* ever since he'd arrived back from Iraq. He respected both Karen's and Frank's privacy where their marriage was concerned. But now Benny was in his clinic and a patient under the clinic's care.

"I can't deny that I was thrilled Teresa agreed to help Benny. But she can't do it alone."

"I know that," Karen agreed.

"You know I don't want to pry, but I can't help but think there is something else going on that is adding to Benny's distress."

Karen's posture stiffened. "You mean at home with Frank and me?"

Dennis sighed. His sister was a private woman. Although they'd always been close, there was a boundary they never crossed. He'd just taken his first step over that invisible line.

"If there is anything you can tell me to share with Teresa about what might be going on at home, either with you and Benny, Frank and Benny or anything else, I think you should do it now. It may help."

Tears welled up in Karen's eyes, and it was hard for Dennis not to jump out of his chair and try to ease his sister's suffering.

"There's so much talk, Dennis. You know how Stockington Falls is."

"Teresa's a professional. You don't even have to confide in me about whatever it is, Karen, if you'd rather wait until Benny is done and tell Teresa directly. Of course, you know I'm here if you do want to tell me anything. I'll leave that up to you. But Teresa should know."

Karen shrugged. "If there is anything *to* tell, you mean."

"Yes."

Karen looked away and fiddled nervously with her hands in her lap. Then she turned to him, her voice almost a whisper. "You know Frank hates talk."

Dennis fought to keep hidden the surge of anger that gripped him. "This isn't about Frank right now. It's about helping Benny. And the only reason people here will talk is because they care."

She sputtered. "Do you really believe that?"

"You and I have known the people of Stockington Falls our whole lives. It's not just a place to live. It's family. That's why I came back."

"Frank thinks…"

"What?"

"He thinks you want to rub in his face that he's not doing as well as you are. That's why he never goes out to your house with me."

"That's his insecurity about the layoff and having to take a job he's not happy with taking."

"I told him you gave up a lot to be here in Stockington Falls with us and that you don't make as much money at the clinic as you could have if you'd stayed in Boston."

"Money has never been what drove me, Karen. You know that."

"Yeah. I know how unhappy you were to be so far away from Stockington Falls. That's why I was thrilled you came home and decided to stay here after your tour in Iraq. I missed you."

Emotion choked him. "Me, too, sis. Just think about it, okay? I'm not going to let up on this. I love you all and want to see you, Frank and Benny get back to where you need to be. Happy again."

That earned him a smile from his sister. He'd gotten through the tough part of the conversation. The rest—actually following through with talking to Teresa—was up to Karen.

"So that takes care of my happiness," Karen said. "What about yours?"

"What about mine?"

Karen rolled her eyes. "You haven't so much as smiled at another woman since Donna left. But I've seen the way you look at Teresa. You like her."

"What's not to like?"

"You're evading the issue."

"I didn't realize there was an issue."

"She said she's not staying in Stockington Falls. She's only going to be here long enough to help Benny. Don't get me wrong. I'm grateful for anything she can do. I just don't want to see you get hurt."

Dennis didn't relish the idea of repeating the pain of a past breakup. And if it were any other time, yeah, he could see trying to pursue a relationship with Teresa. But there were more important things he needed to focus on right now.

"Let's just worry about Benny right now." He didn't want his sister worrying any more than she had to. It would be up to Dennis to worry about his growing feelings for Teresa and what, if anything, he'd do when she ultimately left Stockington Falls.

As she'd expected, Benny's session was uneventful. He'd stared at the ceiling, the window and the empty bookshelf behind Teresa's desk rather than confront his feelings. Every once in a while she was rewarded with a short answer or, more often, a shrug of his shoulder. He was moving a little easier, which meant his body was healing, which was good.

They had a lot of work ahead to help him with

his frame of mind, and she was glad when the session was over, if only to clear her head.

In truth, she hadn't expected much with this visit. Most kids copped an attitude instead of opening up to a stranger. It took time to earn trust, and since Teresa had agreed to sign on for this job, she was going to have to give Benny the time he needed to learn to trust her.

She knew very little about Benny. Even the small amount of information Karen had given her on the phone made Benny seem like a generic kid. What she knew about him could apply to any kid in America. She needed more, and she only hoped that through seeing him interact with others, perhaps his peers, she'd get a better feel for the real Benny. Dennis had mentioned he loved basketball and played at the church community center. She'd have to ask what the protocol was for her to make a visit there. The last thing she wanted to do was intrude on a place teens thought of as a sanctuary.

But she was overthinking. Stockington Falls wasn't Hartford. The kids who went to the church community center didn't necessarily go there as a means of escape, like many of the kids she'd met in Hartford. They may just be there to enjoy good, clean fun.

It didn't take long for her to clean up her work

area, such as it was. There wasn't much in the way of paperwork because it was her first official day.

Once back at the condo at the resort, it didn't take long for Teresa to gather her things and pay her final bill. Vanessa stopped her as she was halfway out the door with her bags, pouting.

"So you're already leaving me?" she asked.

Teresa stopped to talk to her friend and offered up a friendly smile. "I'm not leaving you. I'm just moving across town. We talked about this."

"Of course, but I didn't think you were serious. I certainly didn't think you'd be leaving today. Where did you end up finding a place on such short notice?"

Teresa smirked. Vanessa was going to make more of this than it really was, but she couldn't keep it from her. "Dennis offered me the guesthouse on his property."

Vanessa raised one eyebrow with interest. "Oh, really? Do tell me more."

With a chuckle, Teresa said, "There's nothing to tell. I mentioned needing to find an apartment, and his cottage was empty. End of story."

"You're no fun."

"So you keep reminding me."

"Well, at least I'm not losing you completely. Have lunch here at the resort later in the week?"

Teresa dropped her bags and gave Vanessa a warm squeeze. "Sure thing. I'll give you a call tomorrow, and we can make plans."

In the end, leaving the resort felt a little bittersweet. It wasn't home and she'd never thought of it that way, but she had enjoyed her time there. The atmosphere, while sometimes hectic, was also relaxing.

She met Dennis at the clinic, and they drove the distance to his house on the other side of the town. The winding mountain road was dotted with the open fields of farmland, old red barns that were shut tight for the winter and silos. They passed over another covered bridge that was much shorter and not as spectacular as Abbey Bridge but still pretty with the snow-covered roof and thick wood beams.

Dennis pulled into the long driveway of a colonial two-story home that was mostly hidden from the road by maple trees and pines. It looked like an old New England farmhouse like you'd see on a calendar or in a postcard. Teresa pulled in behind him and parked her sedan in the parking space out back between the main house and the small cottage with two large sliding glass doors and a wide deck overlooking the open backyard.

Fresh snow that hadn't been trampled on covered the yard like a clean blanket, broken only by the path that had been cleared from the house to the parking area, as well as the much shorter path to the cottage.

Dennis got out of the car and slammed his door. "Here it is. Home sweet home."

Teresa grabbed her purse and one of her bags from the backseat. "It's beautiful out here."

"Thanks. My parents' home, the one Karen and I grew up in, is just up the street. They have a condo in Florida and spend their winters there. They won't be back for a few months."

Teresa nodded.

Dennis angled his body and pointed through a patch of pine trees. "The Shepherd Hill Bed and Breakfast is right next door. You can just see it through the trees. So if you get sick of me you can always run over there."

She laughed. "I'm sure I'll be fine here."

He smiled, reached in and grabbed her last bag from the backseat of the car. "Come on, I'll show you around."

She followed him up two steps of the cottage's deck and to the first door, which he quickly opened with the key.

"You'll get a lot of sun during the day. These windows make the cottage passive solar. So you may want to shut the curtains if it ever gets too hot with the stove going."

"Okay."

"The cottage used to be an old barn that I had converted when I came home from Iraq. Having lived here most of my life, I knew the previous owners and mentioned that I'd be interested in buying this place if they ever wanted to sell. They were nice enough to hold the place until I got out of the army."

"Well, you can't beat the locations, especially since it's right up the street from family."

As she walked through the windowed door, Teresa was immediately taken aback. Although it wasn't as lavish as the condo she had at the resort, the cottage was indeed newly renovated and beautifully decorated, with colorful throw pillows and linens contrasting with old Vermont relics and black-and-white pictures hanging on the wall of covered bridges and waterfalls from Stockington Falls.

Teresa's eyes were drawn to the cathedral ceiling, planked with knotty yellow pine and the railing draped with an old quilt that hid what she guessed was a sleeping loft. In the far corner, a compact kitchenette sat next to the narrow wrought-iron spiral staircase that led upstairs. To the right of the stairway was a small potbelly stove and a few stacks of wood waiting to churn out heat.

For all its compact size, the guesthouse was

warm and incredibly inviting—just the kind of place where she could sort out all the things clouding her head.

"I thought you said it was one room," Teresa said, still marveling at the charm of the cottage.

"No walls. You could hardly call upstairs a bedroom. It's more of a loft."

"It's wonderful."

He chuckled, clearly pleased she liked the place.

She glanced at him. "Are you making fun of me, Dennis?"

"Would I do that?" He gave her a mischievous grin.

"Yeah, you would." She laughed, too, enjoying his lighthearted teasing.

"See, you already know me well. Let me get this stove going so you won't freeze to death tonight," he said. "Luckily, the place is small, so it heats up fast."

Dennis moved to the stove, adding logs and kindling to get the fire going. After a few tries with a match, he closed the door and played with the damper until she could feel heat coming from the stove.

This was a different, more relaxed Dennis than she'd seen in the past few days since the accident. She liked seeing him this way. The sound of his boots on the wide-planked flooring and the way he busied himself with his task made him look right at home.

She liked Dennis Harrington. She had from the start. But she'd have to find a way to keep some distance between the two of them. There was no way she was ready—mentally or emotionally—for a romantic relationship. And Dennis was such a good man that he deserved to find someone who wasn't such a mess, someone who had come to Stockington Falls to stay, not just to hide from the "real" world.

When he was done, Dennis turned to her. "I'm afraid there isn't much in the way of supplies here in the cottage."

"No problem. I don't expect you to stock me up. Is the Grocery Mart in town the only store to get supplies around here?"

He made a face. "You'll pay an arm and a leg there for a loaf of bread. It caters mostly to the tourists. The nearest real grocery store is about thirty minutes away."

"Oh."

Her stomach was empty, and she was sure it'd be protesting loudly in a little while if she didn't get something in it soon.

"I guess it's takeout then. I don't suppose you have any pizza places that deliver out here?" She wasn't used to the long country roads and traveling distances to get simple items. The thought of driving an hour round-trip and unpacking groceries tonight wasn't too appealing.

"'Fraid not." He hesitated a second. "Why don't you have dinner with me tonight?"

"Aren't you sick of me yet?"

"Never."

"You say that now, but wait until I'm underfoot all day and encroach on all your quiet here."

"I told you earlier. It's a little too quiet here sometimes. Besides, I like the company."

"It's kind of you, but I haven't even unpacked yet."

"There's time enough for that. Besides, your cupboards are empty. Mine are full of food—well, not full but there's at least enough to pull together a dinner."

She thought back to the little lunch she'd had earlier with Vanessa at the diner. If she was going to be stubborn, it meant she was going to go hungry or be forced to drive back to town to pick something up. She didn't have the energy for that.

"I hadn't thought of how long it would take me to do errands out here. Okay, you win but only because I'm starving. Give me a few minutes to freshen up, and I'll be happy to join you."

Dennis's smile touched his eyes and just about

bowled her over. Teresa was feeling the effects of it long after he turned and walked toward the house, leaving her to watch him amble down the cleared path he'd shoveled.

She was in his house, on his turf. *Lord, what am I doing here?* Her simple conversational words to God were always automatic. Her whole life she'd simply talked to the Lord and knew that He was listening. That hadn't changed, but these days it always gave her pause and was even painful. Was He listening now? Did He forgive her for her part in what happened to Mariah?

Her heart ached just thinking about it. If she couldn't forgive herself, how could she expect that God or anyone else would forgive her?

All she'd wanted when she'd come to Stockington Falls was peace. Dennis had a way of quieting the storm inside her, and she had to wonder if meeting him had been part of God's plan. Having a strong faith had gotten her through most of the trials in her life, helped guide her when she was unsure. But now nothing seemed to make sense to her.

Somewhere in the back of her mind, she knew that she hadn't thought clearly about where she was going and, really, why she was staying. She'd come to Stockington Falls to clear her head of memories, of mistakes she'd made that couldn't be erased. As she stood by the window and watched the door to Dennis's old farmhouse seal tight, she wondered if that was too tall a goal for her to reach.

Chapter Six

"Are you all moved in to the hovel you chose over my lovely resort?"

Teresa was just putting on her boots to walk the short distance from the guesthouse over to Dennis's when Vanessa called.

"I see you're still pouting because I moved out of the condo," Teresa said, balancing the phone against her cheek and shoulder while she used both hands to tie her laces.

"Of course I am. I can't just come over for a quick chat anymore. It was fun having you here. Everyone else is so busy having their own fun that they never have time to just sit and chat."

She had to admit she'd miss Vanessa spontaneously showing up at her door for no reason other than girl talk.

"I told you I'd be by. I won't be tied up every day at the clinic."

"You will be if Dennis is there. You'll be having late-night dinners and romantic lunches."

Teresa laughed. "You're such a romantic, Van."

"At least I'll be able to live vicariously through your romance with Dennis."

With a roll of her eyes, Teresa said, "You're impossible."

Unaffected, Vanessa went on.

"Speaking of Dennis, his sister came by the resort today."

"Karen Dulton was at the resort?"

"Yes."

"What did she want?"

"She was asking about a job at the front desk of the hotel. I was walking by when she was talking to Garrett, the day manager, so I stopped and talked a few minutes and asked how her son was doing. Very pleasant woman. I told her she'd do much better waitressing in the restaurant than sitting behind the front desk. Those waitresses pull in some good money from tips."

Teresa dropped her foot to the ground and thought about the reasons Karen Dulton would have gone all the way to the resort asking for a job when Dennis had told her Karen was already working. Their car was totaled in the accident. She'd need another to be able to take Benny to treatment, and they'd need money to cover the extra expense. But Teresa couldn't help but worry that Karen working a second job would also mean that she wouldn't be there to run interference between Benny and his dad if there continued to be friction between them.

Curious, Teresa asked, "So will she be working in the restaurant?"

"I'll put in a good word for her. I'm sure we can give her a few hours a week to fill in the gaps."

Teresa wasn't sure if that was good or bad. On the one hand, it solved a financial situation that was a drain for the family. On the other, it left Benny open. Karen was the strongest supporter Benny had. Without her being there, and being overworked and tired when she was, it would be hard for her to take an active role in helping Benny adjust to therapy. Maybe she could discuss it with Dennis tonight, over dinner. A glance at her watch reminded her that he was probably waiting for her.

"I need to run, Van," she said.

"I hope it wasn't something I said."

Teresa chuckled. "No." Not in the way Vanessa meant anyway. "I have a dinner date with Dennis tonight."

"Oh, really?" The interest in Vanessa's voice

was unmistakable. "And when were you planning on telling me this?"

"I just told you now. It's no big deal. It saves me a trip to the grocery store tonight. That's all."

"Sure." She sounded unconvinced when Teresa hung up the phone, but Teresa didn't care. Vanessa had a very animated way about her, and she loved reading things that weren't on the page. There was no harm in letting her believe this dinner was a real date. Teresa knew better.

The temperature had dropped considerably since Dennis had arrived home. The wind that had been calm all day had picked up and was now beating against his kitchen window. He glanced out at the snow-filled path leading to the cottage. Teresa was headed over, and the battering wind blew her hair in a tangled mess around her face as she walked.

He'd questioned his motives where Teresa was concerned ever since he'd issued the dinner invitation. He couldn't deny his attraction to Teresa, but he wasn't ready for a relationship. There was no room for it in his life with his work. Besides, he'd made the commitment to stay in Stockington Falls. His family, his friends, his work in the form of the clinic he'd built—it was all here. He couldn't let himself fall for another woman who wasn't planning to stay. Not again.

Dennis stood at the counter over a chopping board covered with sliced scallions and carrots and waited for Teresa to make her way to the door. Teresa knocked lightly on the frozen windowpane before pushing through, not waiting for his response. He smiled, liking the fact that she already felt comfortable enough with him not to wait for a response. Perhaps she'd seen through the window that he was deep in his cutting task and decided not to disturb his momentum. Either way, it felt comfortable. The people he knew in Stockington Falls didn't stand on formalities, and that small move made it feel like Teresa fit in to his lifestyle here just a bit more.

He looked up when the door opened, and a gust of wind and snow propelled her into the warm house.

"That was quick," he said.

Teresa shook off the snow from her coat before coming in and closing the door behind her. Even the short walk across the yard must have been chilly by the looks of how she eagerly absorbed the warmth of being in Dennis's house by rubbing her hands. She'd never stepped foot in his house before, but here she was, slipping out of her wool coat as if this house was familiar. It felt odd. There hadn't been a woman over for dinner since Donna.

"I hope you're hungry," Dennis said, still engrossed in slicing and dicing. He didn't need a distraction that would end up with him losing a finger.

When he finished his task, he turned to look at her and smiled. She'd changed out of the casual pants she'd been wearing earlier and had put on dressy sweater and long denim skirt. She wore leather boots with a low heel. The height of the heel was hardly enough to help her reach Dennis's height, but it did make her look taller.

And she looked beautiful. He grabbed her coat and hung it up on the coatrack by the door.

"Smells good. I'm a little hungry. Can I help with anything?"

"You can pour us some drinks, if you're thirsty. They're chilling in the fridge."

She opened the refrigerator and pulled out two bottles of root beer as Dennis rummaged through a cabinet for some glasses.

"Should I take my boots off?" she asked.

With his hand deep in the cabinet, he turned to her. "No, unless you're not comfortable in them."

She glanced at his feet. He wore no shoes or socks, as was usual for him despite the chill outside. He'd changed out of the clothes he'd worn to the clinic and now wore military fatigues and a comfortable T-shirt.

"I think I'm going to need a bottle opener for these bottles," she said. "They're not twist-off tops."

"It's made by a local company. Good stuff. I have a bottle opener in the drawer here." He began rummaging through an all-purpose drawer filled with items that didn't have a better place to be stored.

Dennis handed her the bottle opener and then the glasses. She sat at the table and dropped the glasses in front of the plates that were already set out for dinner.

Taking in a deep whiff of the aroma filling the kitchen, she asked, "What's on tonight's menu?"

"Chicken fajitas."

She arched an eyebrow. "Wow. I'm impressed."

Dennis chuckled as he glanced her way, slightly embarrassed because he'd never made chicken fajitas before and wasn't all that certain how they were going to turn out. Turning his attention to the cutting board, he said, "I wouldn't be until after you had a chance to sample my culinary talents. Or lack of them. I am not much good in the kitchen. Don't expect what you've been accustomed to at the resort."

"Well, let's face it. Jacques is the best. But if you're not that great in the kitchen, what made you think you could whip this up?"

He shrugged. "Cammie just gave me the recipe this afternoon and insisted even *I* couldn't mess it up."

She smirked. "When in doubt, ask Cammie?"

He shrugged. "Something like that. She was happy to help, though. Whether or not I mess it up remains to be seen though."

The clap-clap-clap of the knife against the wooden cutting board made the sudden lag in conversation glaring. Silence made a thick wall between them, which Teresa quickly worked to tear down.

"How is Cammie doing?"

"Coping like she always does, throwing herself into her work." He shook his head, trying not to worry. Cammie was strong. But even she had a breaking point, and Dennis didn't want to see it. "She practically lives at the clinic now when she's not with John and Drew. Not that she didn't before, but now it seems worse."

Teresa poured a glass of root beer and placed it on the counter next to Dennis.

"She doesn't seem all that open to talking with me," she said. "But does she talk to you about… you know, the accident? Her feelings about losing Molly?"

He stopped cutting. "Not at all," he said, feeling the sudden weight of his concern over Cammie settle in on him. "Except that she's very worried about Drew right now."

"Molly's son? Quite frankly, I am, too."

"Under the circumstances, he seems to be doing well. I noticed you had a talk with John Peterson earlier when he brought Drew in."

Teresa nodded. "From what little I could gather from Drew this afternoon, he doesn't remember the accident at all. Or doesn't want to remember it. It will be a while before he's able to process all that has happened to him and what he's really feeling. I'm only sorry John Peterson decided against counseling."

"Yeah, I was surprised about that. I don't think he subscribes to the same belief as Benny's dad on that point."

"You're right. He did seem open to the idea. I think he's just not ready himself. I told him that I was going to be in town for a little while and if he changed his mind he could contact me at the clinic. When he's ready, I'm sure he'll take Drew."

"That's good to know. I only wish Cammie would reconsider talking to you."

Teresa's eyes widened. "You talked to her about it already?"

"Yes, but…"

"It can't be forced, Dennis, which is why I'm not

sure I can be of help to Benny, either. He doesn't seem at all open to talking to me."

Teresa cleared her throat before taking a quick sip of root beer, then ran her tongue over her lips before speaking. "It's not important that any of them talk to a counselor per se as long as there is someone they can trust and open up to. Cammie is lucky to have you look after her like that. She shouldn't be alone if she's suppressing her grief."

Dennis snapped his head up to look at her, wondering where she was going with her line of thinking. "I think you should be saying that to Mac, not me. He's the one who has been spending all his free time checking in on her. And believe me, he has his hands full as it is right now."

"Mac?"

"Daniel MacKenzie, Stockington Fall's chief of police."

"Oh, yes, Dan."

Dennis's interest was piqued. "You're on a first-name basis with the chief of police? Should I be jealous?"

Teresa tossed him a grin. "We met at the clinic that first day I was brought in—before you examined my ankle. I guess it's protocol to check out klutzy guests at the hotel. Cammie and Dan were still an item then. I've seen him around town a few times since."

"Ah."

She chuckled and baited him a little. "He's kind of cute, though, especially with that Southern accent of his. I hear he's from Memphis."

Dennis gave her a sidelong glance, mindful of the pang of jealousy that punched him in the gut. "Yeah, but I don't think I want to talk any more about Daniel MacKenzie."

She laughed then and playfully smacked his arm. "You men are so childish whenever anyone says something nice about another man."

Only if the "anyone" is you, Dennis thought. He shook his head, serious for a moment. "I know how crazy Mac is about Cammie. Cammie and Mac had a thing going for a while, but for some reason it didn't work out. She needs him. She just won't let herself. I'm glad he's as stubborn as she is on this issue, though."

She eased back in the chair. It really wasn't Dennis's business who Teresa Morales was interested in personally, but it surprised him that he felt a little green with the mention of Mac's name, and he didn't really want to bring the other man into the conversation further. But if he wanted to give Benny the best shot at recovery, he needed to be open with Teresa about everything.

"Mac stopped in again today and asked a bunch of questions about Benny and Drew and what they may have said. He spoke with Allie Pryor, too. Seems every time he talks to someone more questions come up."

Intrigued, Teresa asked, "Such as?"

Dennis shrugged. "There were a whole list of things going against anyone who was on the road that night. Mac is very thorough. I'm sure he wants to make sure the police report is as complete as possible. The road conditions, blinding snow, the party mood and any drinking done in excess probably contributed equally."

Teresa's eyes widened. "Benny insists he wasn't drunk. I haven't seen the police report yet, but I'm sure that will be in there."

"His blood alcohol level was very low. He wasn't drunk, but he did have a little to drink, which I'm not happy about at all." Dennis shook his head. "It's always been a worry of mine. His paternal grandfather was an alcoholic. I don't know why he'd even touch the stuff."

"What about Karen's husband?"

"Frank never used to drink. Since I've been home from Iraq, I've wondered, though. He seems different. Their relationship has changed. I thought maybe it was just the stress of what's been happening with Benny. Benny has pretty much retreated into himself since the suicide attempts. Did Karen fill you in on those?"

"Briefly. He cut himself the first time. Frank insisted it was an accident."

Dennis drew in a deep breath. That attempt was before he'd come home from Iraq. When he'd heard the story, he didn't believe Frank's explanation. It was only confirmed when he saw the scar on Benny's arm. Accidents happen but not like that.

"The second attempt was with his dirt bike last summer, right?" Teresa asked.

"Yeah. I was there for that one, and no amount of excuses from Frank could change what I saw in my mind. He was aiming for the tree."

"I believe both attempts, while very serious, were a cry for help," Teresa suggested. "Benny could have chosen a much more definitive way to do the deed. He didn't. The doctor at the emergency room that night suggested counseling and even meds, which I think could be a good course of action since Benny is still so clearly in a serious state of mind."

"Frank refused." Dennis shook his head.

"That's enough to upset any mother and cause friction in a marriage. Have you talked to Benny about the drinking?"

"Yes, and he flat-out denied it, even though the blood test shows otherwise. In the end, he's got to learn on his own. Kids sometimes do the exact opposite of what you teach them. I try to focus on positive outlets down at the community center, get the kids involved in sports and something to think of other than getting into trouble. But I'm sure you know from working in Hartford that guidance like that can only go so far."

"True. The rest is up to them to make good choices."

Dennis thought a moment. "None of it makes any sense though. Benny keeps talking about the 'other' truck."

"There was another vehicle involved in the accident besides Benny's and Molly's, right?"

"Allie Pryor's Trooper. She hasn't remembered much of the accident until today. She was knocked unconscious after the accident and only came to when rescue workers pulled her from the car. She's been fuzzy about the details of that night, which is normal. She may never remember them."

"Really? She's still at the clinic then?"

Dennis nodded, pushing aside the chopping board piled high with vegetables.

"I'll be releasing her tomorrow. Her injuries weren't all that severe, and she's doing well. She could have gone home that next morning, but I hesitated because she's a widow and lives alone. With head injuries of any kind, it's best to have someone there to watch the patient. Her brother, Andrew, is coming back from law school to stay with her for a few days until she's better able to stay alone."

"Then I should talk with her tomorrow before she leaves. I need to talk to Cammie, too, although I think it's probably best that I wait a bit. When is Molly's funeral?"

"Later in the week."

Teresa nodded. "It'll do until then."

"What is it?"

She waved him off. "Nothing urgent. Just something Benny said that doesn't make sense to me."

"But Cammie wasn't there at the scene. I called her into the clinic when I was called by the dispatcher. What would she have to offer?"

"I don't know. Maybe nothing."

He smiled. "I'm glad to see you're really embracing this. I like that."

Teresa rolled her eyes. "I'm not out to save the world, Dennis. I just think Allie probably saw what happened and can help me sort things out with Benny. Cammie may have some insight into Molly that may be useful. She was Molly's best friend and knew her."

"What does knowing Molly have to do with the accident?"

"Like I said, maybe nothing. But it's important that I find out as much information about the

accident as possible so I can counter Benny's nega-
tivity and blame. If he relies only on his memory
or imagination of what happened, he may continue
to blame himself for things that weren't his fault,
and I won't be able to help him move on."

"Then I think it's a good idea that you have a
talk with them. Benny shouldn't have to carry guilt
for what happened. Driving over Abbey Bridge
during the daytime can be a challenge when too
many cars are involved. The conditions on New
Year's Eve made it much worse."

Teresa shook her head. "Benny's so confused.
He won't tell me about what drove him the other
times he tried to hurt himself, what was going on
in his life. So I have no idea if this incident is even
related to his past depression."

The worried look etched Dennis's strong and
handsome features once again. "He didn't say anything at all?"

"All he said is that it's all his fault Chuck is hurt,
but he didn't cause Molly's accident. I keep thinking there's more than what meets the eye here.
There was enough going on with the weather that
night to cause a pileup without laying blame in any
one direction."

Dennis opened the glass front cabinet door above
the counter and pulled out a can of olive oil. He

sprinkled oil on the cast-iron frying pan already settled over the flaming burner and pushed the cut pieces of raw chicken into the pan.

"Want me to heat the tortillas?" she asked then took a sip of her root beer.

"Have you ever done it before?"

"Once or twice," she said, her lips stretching into a grin Dennis found infinitely appealing.

"Then you're light-years ahead of me."

She chuckled. "You really don't cook often."

"No, I'm usually satisfied with a frozen TV dinner or takeout from the Twin Falls Café across from the clinic. Most nights I call ahead to Louise to make up a plate of whatever is on special. I never had to cook while I was in Iraq, and Donna used to do all the cooking before."

"Donna?"

"My former fiancée."

Her breath hitched. "You never mentioned you were engaged to be married."

"Does it matter?"

"No, just noteworthy."

He glanced at her and remembered a time when something as small as standing in the kitchen brought back memories of Donna. But now he searched for some remnants of regret or sadness and found that they weren't there. Instead, he reached over and cupped her cheek. He flipped a lock of her hair behind her ear, letting his fingers pause on the flesh beneath her ear. He was over Donna…but was he ready to risk his heart on Teresa?

"I think of it as a small blip in the grand scheme of things."

"Your engagement was a blip?" she asked skeptically. "Oh, that's romantic. I wonder why she split?"

"What makes you think it was her who left?"

"Okay, bad assumption."

He shrugged, trying not to let the fact that Teresa was dead-on correct get the better of him. "She *was* the one to leave me. But it was mostly Stockington Falls she didn't want. She asked me to go with her when she left."

"And you didn't run after her."

Dennis returned to sautéing vegetables. "No, I didn't run after her."

"Were you together long?"

"Yes. All through med school, in fact. But the strange thing was when I came back from Iraq, it was glaringly clear that our visions for the future were very different. To a certain extent I knew that before I left on my tour. I thought we'd overcome it, find a way around it, whatever."

"But that didn't happen?"

"I'm not career military. I'm in the army reserves

and was called out for a tour in Iraq. I didn't mind being called. I wanted to do what I could for the soldiers there. Donna and I had been separated for fifteen months by the time I returned. She was fully entrenched in her job at Mass General and wanted nothing to do with the things I had realized were really important to me. We tried the long-distance relationship thing for a while, but it didn't work. In the end, it didn't hurt as much as it would have if we didn't respect each other so much."

"So you called off the engagement just like that?"

"Pretty much. She got a job offer in D.C. and wanted me to go with her. I asked her to come here, which she did for about a month to see what had such a hold on me. The clinic was almost open at that point. One morning, she just woke up and said goodbye, and that was it."

Teresa's mouth had dropped open during his story. When she became aware of it, she lifted the gold-rimmed glass to her lips to take a sip of drink.

"It sounds very…"

"Adult." He practically spat out the word as if it tasted bitter, and there had been days it had. But since he'd met Teresa, it amazed him how much those bitter feelings had faded.

* * *

Teresa listened to Dennis with interest. It amazed her just how open he was being with her. Once people found out she was a therapist, they usually closed off from her, even the ones who came to her for counseling. Everyone has painful things they want to hide, and everyone was afraid of how much they might actually spill while talking to a professional. But this was more than just uncharacteristic openness that she was getting from Dennis. She'd never known a man to be so transparent and feel so comfortable with it the way Dennis seemed to be.

"You sound as though the behavior bothers you more than losing someone who was important to you."

He shrugged, tossing the vegetables into the skillet. Teresa decided not to tell him he should be sautéing instead of stirring. Seeing the vulnerable side of Dennis as a man instead of the practical medical doctor was worth more than perfectly sautéed chicken and vegetables.

She couldn't remember the last time she'd been that open with anyone. Even before everything had fallen apart in Hartford, Teresa hadn't really had anyone she felt she could confide in. Would she still have run from Hartford if there had been someone there she could turn to? If someone like Dennis had been there, would it have made a difference? She didn't know. She was the one people came to for answers, yet she had none for herself.

"I think that was the whole problem. We were too professional, too courteous with each other. We respected each other's position and didn't cross the boundaries. Except once."

"Only once?"

"Yeah, if you can believe that. I pressed her to stay in Stockington Falls. We'd met in Boston during our residency. I told her I couldn't stay there. She knew that. I'd already decided Stockington Falls was where I wanted to start my practice, but I wonder if I'd ever really shared that with her. When I left for Iraq, I asked her to marry me and come live here."

"She must have wanted to or she never would have said yes to your proposal."

He gave her a wry grin. "She did say no, at first. I was pretty persuasive. And being young and in love, we didn't look far enough ahead. But I think she said yes against her better judgment just as I proposed somehow knowing it wasn't going to end up the way I envisioned. Anyway, it only seemed fair to respect her wish to make a difference practicing medicine in D.C. instead of a small community like Stockington Falls."

"Any regrets?"

"You reach thirty-six years of age and you've achieved some sense of who you are and some measure of success. I don't mean monetarily but personally and professionally." He glanced at her quickly, then back to the frying pan. "Success is measured in many more ways than just in a career."

"I think you've done a tremendous job here. From what Vanessa told me, Stockington Falls never had a medical facility before you started the clinic."

His smile was slight but filled with pride that made it seem much bigger than it actually was. "It's one of the reasons I wanted to come back here after I left the army. I'd been gone for almost ten years. I knew I couldn't live in D.C., which is where Donna is now. This is where I'd always planned to be. Funny though, I'd always pictured myself at this age with at least a few kids running around." He shrugged. "God had other plans, I guess."

Teresa chuckled. "You're not ancient, Dennis. You could still have a family. There's plenty of time."

His gaze bored into her, strong and meaningful. "What about you, Teresa? Have you ever thought about having children?"

Her jaw dropped open and closed in a millisecond

as she thought carefully about what she would say. Her mouth suddenly felt like cotton. "I guess I've always thought it would happen sometime in the future. Most of the time I think of the kids at the high school as being my children."

"Your work in Hartford, it's important to you?"

"Yes, very much. It always was, anyway. I put my heart and soul into my work for the past ten years."

"Then what made you come running to Stockington Falls?"

She stared for a few seconds, not quite knowing what to say. She didn't want to talk about her reasons for coming, although it was clear Dennis knew there *was* something that had made her run. Was she really such an open book that he knew she'd not just come to Stockington Falls for a simple change?

Of course, his conversation with Spencer had probably given him more reason to suspect it even if he didn't have the facts to go along with his assumption. Dennis was a smart man, and a simple check of the archives from the *Hartford Courant* on the internet was probably all he needed to put two and two together. Still, if he knew the truth, he didn't push, as if he was waiting for her to make the first move in telling him what really happened.

She wasn't ready to go there. While she couldn't deny that she felt quite at home with Dennis, her wounds were still raw, and she needed to nurture them a little while longer before uncovering them in front of anyone.

Lord, will it always be this hard?

"That's almost ready, isn't it?" she finally asked.

Dennis averted his gaze—not noticeably, but she knew… He'd wanted an answer, wanted her to open up to him the way he had to her. And the low rumbling sound he made showed his disappointment that she hadn't.

He nodded his head in answer to her questions. Dinner was almost done and so was the conversation about Hartford and her reasons for being in Vermont.

It was only then that Teresa realized she'd practically gone the entire conversation without doing her part for dinner. She'd been so totally engrossed in Dennis's story that she'd forgotten her offer to heat the tortillas. "Just give me a second to get these ready."

He grabbed a skillet from the lower cabinet and dropped it on the burner next to the other pan. He was inches from her in the tiny workspace. There was a whole, wide-open kitchen behind them, but they were standing close.

It took Teresa a second or two to realize Dennis had killed the flame under the frying pan he'd used to cook the chicken and vegetables. He just stood there, staring down at her while she flipped the tortilla.

She braved a glance up at him, the all-built-for-serious-business Dennis Harrington. No matter what he was doing, he always looked strong and capable.

His voice was low when he spoke. "Are you afraid, Teresa?"

She moistened her lips. "Of what?"

"Of working with Benny."

She sighed. "I'm okay, Dennis. You don't have to worry about me freaking out on Benny or running through the halls of the clinic again." She pressed her hand to her face as shame crashed in with the memory of it all. "I know I shouldn't have done that."

"That's not what I meant."

She snapped her gaze at him.

"What did you mean?"

"You reacted to Benny and the situation. Yeah, I get that, and I know you'll be on your guard. If that part was going to be a problem, you wouldn't have come back and agreed to help him. I'm not worried about you quitting. I'm worried about *you*. He's my nephew, and I know how difficult he can be. Are you up for it?"

She chuckled. "You mean teenage attitude? Piece of cake."

"Lady, you're one strong woman," he said with a deep chuckle that was balm to her soul. "Something tells me you'll give him a run for his money. And look at you."

She slowly lifted her gaze to him, saw his shaking head.

"What's wrong with me?" She glanced down at her sweater and long skirt as if she'd find something glaringly wrong with the way she'd dressed. She'd worn her shirt right side out. Her clothes were clean.

Dennis tipped her chin up with his finger.

"You look incredibly cute right now, but you're burning the tortillas."

She gasped and pulled the flat pan off the burner before flipping the tortilla. It was indeed on its way to being burned.

"Then stop distracting me," she said.

Dennis gave her a teasing grin. "Was your takeout of choice Chinese or pizza?"

He had her pegged.

"Okay, I'm not much of a cook myself. I admit

it. Subs at the corner sub shop. Stop distracting me from what I'm doing."

"Okay but only because I'm hungry. I won't distract you any more with conversation until we sit to eat."

She let Dennis go on thinking it was the conversation that had her burning the tortillas. Only she knew it was the distraction of the man whose company she was in.

Chapter Seven

They did, indeed, continue their conversation through dinner, but Teresa was glad that the subject was far away from Hartford. Neither one of them had trouble finding things to talk about—so much so that Teresa was surprised when she glanced at the clock on her way to putting the dirty dishes in the sink and it read 9:30 p.m.

As Dennis loaded the dishwasher, she made coffee; then they settled on the overstuffed sofa in his living room. Quite a bit larger than the small living area of the cottage, Dennis's living room was decorated in a soothing palette of earth tones and vintage pieces of furniture. She wasn't sure if they were antiques, but they blended well together and made the room look homey.

The granite fireplace that commanded the opposite wall from the sofa had the small glow of fading embers. Dennis has started the fire earlier, but it had died down from neglect during their dinner. As she curled up on the sofa with a warm cup of coffee in her hand, she watched as Dennis stoked the fire back to life.

He'd pushed the sleeves of his white shirt up on his arms as he worked, revealing a nasty scar on the inside flesh just below his elbow. She'd seen scars similar to this on troubled students over the years, usually self-inflicted or the result of a knife fight.

In the dim light, the scar could easily be overlooked, but now that she'd found it, Teresa had a hard time keeping her curiosity over it in check.

"Did you get that scar playing sports when you were a kid?" she asked, hoping it was from something as simple as childhood athletics and not a result of something that had happened while he was in the army.

His eyes drifted from the fire he'd just set a log on to her, his gaze lingering on her lips, then her eyes, then moved to the scar on his arm. "I was a resident at Boston General when I got this wound."

Her stomach sank. "Oh, that can't have been good."

"No, it wasn't," he said, pushing the fire screen shut and settling onto the sofa next to her.

"Do you mind me asking how it happened?"

"A kid just out of high school came in the E.R. one night. He was higher than the moon and thought he was Marilyn Manson or John Lennon or who only knows what."

He shifted to his side, bringing her legs up so they stretched across his on the sofa. She wiggled her toes as he rested his hands on her feet. As he caressed them, she sank back against the back of the sofa and listened to his story.

"The guy never really had a chance," he said softly. "I never like saying that, but it was true. It was almost as if he was already gone the moment they wheeled him in on the gurney."

"If he was that far gone, how did he manage to hurt you?"

Dennis sighed heavily, his hand stopping in mid-motion on the heel of her foot but remaining in place. "It was as if he'd come to life on a surge of adrenaline—just all of the sudden. Drugs will do that. One minute he was down and the next he was slipping a hunting knife from his boot and swinging. I wasn't what he was aiming for. Truth of it is, I don't even think he could see me. But the blade found its way in my arm before the police officer who'd come in with the EMTs restrained him. I was lucky this is all he hit. For a while, I thought I was going to lose the use of my arm. But I was luckier than him."

Teresa groaned softly. "Don't tell me."

Dennis cocked his head to one side. "You work in the school system. I'm sure you can figure it out." He shook his head. "That was a long time ago. Unfortunately, things like that don't just happen in the city. I've seen that very thing happen right here. Although, thankfully, not as often. What makes it harder is that I know most of the kids here."

"Is that why you wanted to come back to Stockington Falls? To help people you know instead of dealing with strangers?"

"People are people wherever you go. In Iraq, it didn't matter to me if I was treating a soldier or an Iraqi who couldn't understand a word I was saying. If they needed help, I was there. But coming home was different. I wasn't just a tourist coming here to ski like everyone else. I saw there was a need that wasn't being filled, and it was going to take someone who loved the place and loved the people here to fill it. I guess you could say it was my wake-up call from the Lord. There was no reason I couldn't make as much a difference in Stockington Falls as I could in Boston."

"Or Washington, D.C.?"

He thought a second. "D.C. was never really an option for me. My relationship with Donna was already too distant for it to be a real consideration. What about you?"

She untangled her legs from his lap and dropped them to the floor, suddenly uncomfortable with the change of direction. "Hartford isn't D.C., but it's not Stockington Falls, either."

"You seem to like it here."

"What's not to like? It's beautiful."

He thought a second. "It has a different rhythm. That's not for everyone."

"True enough. Vanessa has said as much."

Dennis's face showed amusement. "Ah, Vanessa. I forgot you two have become quick friends."

Teresa chuckled. "What's wrong with that?"

"Nothing, other than the fact that you are like night and day."

"Yeah, my dark hair and her bleached blond hair. She's nice, though. Easy to talk to."

"She stays for Hal."

"Maybe she loves it here. Or am I trampling on doctor/patient privilege?"

Dennis chuckled quietly. "Nothing about Vanessa is ever kept privileged. She's an open book. But she has a good heart. She and Hal never had any kids of their own, so she donates some time down at the community center with the little ones. She makes it sound like it's no big deal when she talks about it. But I think it's more important to her than she lets on."

Teresa thought about it a second. "I can see that about her."

"You could do the same thing. Make a difference here in Stockington Falls."

"Working at the community center and at the clinic?"

Teresa stared at him thoughtfully, afraid of seeing any more meaning in what he was saying. He didn't elaborate further.

"I guess I don't see myself in either extreme on a permanent basis," she finally said. "Not anymore, anyway."

Dennis remained quiet a few moments before he added, "Benny is going to need a lot of looking after. He's going to fight you on it. And Frank will, too."

"I know. And I'll do my best. But I won't be the one to give Benny everything he needs. Or what your sister needs either, for that matter. I'm here for the time being, Dennis, to help Benny get on the right track—get him thinking about his future in a positive way. But in the long run they're all going to need family counseling. Benny and Karen are going to need to find strength."

"My sister has a strong faith in God." Dennis eased out a slow breath. "I guess I'll just have to be satisfied with that for now and take things one day at a time."

It was good to know that Karen had her faith to get her through these troubled times in her family. Before long, Teresa would be going back to Hartford. She wasn't going to be here to make sure that Benny didn't suffer the same fate as Mariah.

Teresa spent her first night in the guesthouse mulling over her conversation with Dennis. She woke the next morning to a cold floor and frost on the windows.

Putting her wool socks on, she made her way down the spiral staircase to the woodstove. Embers were still glowing when she opened the woodstove door, but there was no flame. Hopefully, putting a log or two on top of the embers would make the fire burn to life. Dennis had been right about how quickly the cottage heated up once the fire got going. She got to work with the stove and then traipsed across the cold floor to check out the cabinet situation.

Empty. She was going to need to make a grocery store run before she did anything. There wasn't a donut shop on every corner in Stockington Falls, so she couldn't just run out for a cup of coffee and then come back home. She quickly jotted down a few items on a piece of paper to remember to get later when she was at the store.

The stove started pumping out heat, and Teresa took advantage of that warmth to rub her hands together. That was when she smelled the smoke. Looking down, Teresa panicked as smoke seeped out through the stove door and into the small space.

The smoke filled the room, making her cough as she made her way to the window to open it and get some fresh air in the cottage. As she pushed the curtains back, she panicked once again.

Dennis's SUV was gone. That discovery was met with a mixture of relief and distress. She liked Dennis's company, and she found herself at ease in a way she hadn't felt in the presence of a man in a long time. She certainly could get used to having him around.

But right now, Dennis wasn't here, and she had no idea how to get the smoke out of the cottage. She wasn't a country girl. She'd never even been a Girl Scout. She picked up her cell phone and used the one survival skill she knew. She called 911.

Stockington Falls fire chief, Carlos Garcia, still had a smile on his face when he walked out of the cottage and came up to the window of her sedan. Teresa had spent the past thirty minutes sitting in her heated car in her pajamas and a ski parka while Carlos and his crew checked the woodstove and chimney pipe to see if she'd had a chimney fire.

"It's all set, Ms. Morales. You just put too much

wood in the stove and didn't give the pipe enough time to heat the air before the stove heated up."

"But the smoke is supposed to rise," she said, feeling like an idiot when Carlos's face widened into a bigger smile.

"It will. But a fire has to build gradually or it gets too hot in the stove too quick."

Dressed in his fireman gear, Carlos used his hands to demonstrate how smoke should flow through the chimney.

"You see, the smoke will only rise if there's hot air in the pipe to suck it out. It's like a vacuum really. If there is too much cold air in the pipe and too much heat in the stove, the smoke won't get sucked up the pipe, and will take whatever path it can to escape. In this case, it seeped out of the stove and into the cottage. Some kindling or a smaller log would have prevented it from happening."

"So there's no chimney fire."

"No, ma'am."

She covered her face with her hand as humiliation flooded her. "I can't believe I did that on the first morning here."

Carlos laughed. "I'm pretty sure Dennis likes that woodsy smell you're going to have in there for a while until things air out."

Teresa couldn't help but laugh. "I'm going to look like an idiot when I tell Dennis about this."

"Don't worry. Dennis has a sense of humor."

"Thank you, Carlos. I really appreciate you coming out here this morning."

"Anytime. Dennis must have been up at the crack of dawn. He's already shoveled you a path and cleared the driveway. It made it easier to get the fire truck up his driveway. Tell him I said thanks."

"I will."

She got out of her car and waved as the firemen pulled out of the driveway, already dreading her conversation with Dennis.

Glancing at her watch, she saw that it was quarter past nine. Dennis *must* have been up early in order to shovel.

Strange. She hadn't heard him. He had to have left early for the clinic.

She went inside the guesthouse and took in a deep breath.

"Yep. Woodsy smell. You're in Vermont, Teresa, not Hartford."

Shaking her head as she pulled the curtains shut, Teresa abandoned the idea of getting the stove going again until Dennis was home to show her how to use it properly. The sun was rising in the east, showing a beautiful day on the way. She opened the curtains in an effort to let the sun in and hopefully give some heat to the cottage during the day while she was gone.

She needed to get moving so she could tell Dennis about her mishap.

Yeah, right. She'd like to say that she was seeking him out to tell him about the stove fire, but she was drawn to him, and it didn't take much of an excuse on her part to find a reason to see him.

It had been a long time since she'd been interested in any man at all. Most of the men she'd met in her life were full of ambition. Of course, there was nothing wrong with a healthy dose of ambition, and Teresa could certainly see that in Dennis as well. He'd made quite a showing here in Stockington Falls, filling in a gap that was much needed in a community that made its living on tourism.

But this was…different.

She looked up at the ceiling. "How's that for clarity, Lord?" The space she'd craved when she left Hartford only brought her more turmoil.

She'd only been in Vermont for a little over a month, but already Teresa could tell the difference between those who were just passing through and those who had dug in their roots. It was evident that even when Dennis had been away at med school and served in Iraq, that his feet had been firmly planted here where there were people he loved.

She envied Dennis for that. The slow pace with which he took in life around him was something she didn't see in Hartford and had never felt herself. Everything was larger than life where she'd come from—fast and immediate, much like a flash fire. It burned bright, and then it was gone.

She wondered what it would be like to be in a relationship with someone who'd grown up and lived in a world so vastly different from her own. Opposites attracted, but could that attraction, coupled with the differences, be long lasting? Would it grow into something more?

Regardless, being with Dennis had already proven to be a learning experience. It had begun to open her eyes about just how closed off she was in seeing simple everyday things, like Dennis throwing sand on the ground when it was icy.

Sure, she knew they did those winter tasks back in Hartford. But that simple chore was already complete by the time she'd make her way to the front door of the condo and out to school.

Living like she had, it was hard to notice the little things. She hadn't. But she had noticed them last night. Dennis liked to walk around the house in his bare feet with no socks, even in this unbelievable cold weather. It had to be a hair above freezing outside. Wiggling her toes, she recalled how she'd put on a heavy pair of wool socks herself when she'd climbed out of bed this morning and realized just how cold the floor could be.

Teresa had been so busy with her life in Hartford that she probably would have missed something simple like that before. She couldn't help but wonder if she would have noticed what was going on with Mariah if what had happened in Hartford had instead happened here in Stockington Falls.

There wasn't time to dwell on it. She couldn't right the wrongs of her past, and no amount of turning it over in her mind was going to change it. She had an early appointment with Benny at the clinic. Since the family was down to one car, Karen Dulton was going to drop Benny off at the clinic, and Dennis would drive him home when the session was done. The high school students were still on Christmas vacation. Benny hadn't had a chance to talk to many of the other kids at school since the accident. But all that would change on Monday, and she wanted to make sure he was prepared.

After a quick shower and change into something more appropriate than blue jeans, Teresa made her way to town. Vermont was ready for inclement weather. The roads were plowed and mostly bare of snow, but the snowbanks on the side of the road made navigating narrow roads nerve-racking. She took her time on the winding turns where she knew black ice could catch her off guard.

It had been black ice that had caused the accident that killed Mariah's boyfriend, David. Teresa gripped the steering wheel and kept her eyes peeled on the road ahead, knowing that attentiveness alone wouldn't be enough if she hit a patch of ice or if a deer ran in front of her car.

Dennis drove a four-wheel-drive vehicle. Now she understood why. Her little sedan didn't handle these side roads quite the same what they did on I-95 in Connecticut.

She slowed as she reached Abbey Bridge, being careful to check to make sure another vehicle hadn't already gone into the covered bridge. There was barely enough room for two small cars to pass each other while going over the bridge on dry pavement, let alone an SUV and larger sedan. Benny had said the roads were slippery and that Molly's car had careened off the inside barrier. The angry scar of splintered wood had been patched over enough with fresh boards to prevent anyone else from breaking through and plunging to the water below. The sight of it gave Teresa a chill.

The road on the bridge was dry. Even with the heavy snowfall New Year's Eve, surely inside the bridge the road should have been free of snow. She'd have to remember to ask Dennis about the conditions of the road and whether ice buildup inside the bridge was normal when the temperature dropped.

As she came through the other side, she was startled by a man walking onto the bridge on foot. She pumped her brakes, afraid she'd slide on the snow buildup the wind was blowing into the mouth of the bridge. She caught her breath as she recognized the person walking.

Rolling down her window, she said, "Daniel MacKenzie, you scared the daylights out of me."

Teresa had met the Stockington Falls chief of police on several occasions while staying at the resort. He was still new to the area by Vermont standards. For that matter, so was Vanessa, and she'd been at the resort nearly twenty years. Only people born and raised here were considered native.

"Sorry, Teresa. I was just making sure the patch on the bridge was finished. I don't want anyone to accidentally fall through."

"I appreciate that. The thought had crossed my mind."

"Where are you headed?"

"Over to the clinic. I need to talk to Dennis."

He nodded, and although questions crossed his face, he chose to keep them silent.

"She's doing fine," Teresa offered, knowing he was thinking of Cammie.

Mac shrugged. "She's always *fine*. I'd like to see for myself."

"Then why don't you come with me? I'm sure she's there."

He shook his head and stood tall. Teresa had to crane her neck to look at him as she sat in the car.

"Of course she's there. But Cammie's a stubborn woman. She won't take my calls. She doesn't think she needs anyone but will be there for anyone else who's in need."

He drew in a deep breath, clearly frustrated.

"I'll keep an eye on her," Teresa said, smiling warmly.

A gust of wind that had gotten caught in the tunnel of the bridge whipped against her car, chilling her. Her heater was on full blast, but the hot air escaped as soon as it blew out of the front vents.

Mac tapped the roof of her car and said, "You'd better get going. There's going to be a shift change at the resort soon, which means a lot of traffic down here."

"I certainly don't want to get caught in that. There's enough traffic with the skiers. When you have some time, though, I'd like to talk to you a little about the accident."

"What about?"

"Just some details. I'm trying to figure out a time-line of events. I'm hoping it will help Benny."

"Dennis's nephew?"

"Yes. If there is anything you can add to what he told me about the accident, I'd appreciate hearing it."

"I'll be interested in hearing more about what he has to say, too. He wasn't too forthcoming the night of the accident, although that's to be expected. He was worried about his friend. I'll be in my office later today if you want to drop by. I have the police report back from the state police. We can have a look at it together."

They said their goodbyes, and Teresa rolled up her window. Enclosed in the car, her heater was quicker to warm the air around her. She made a mental note of Mac's comment about the shift change. The accident on New Year's Eve happened just before midnight. Perhaps the added traffic along with the road conditions were what caused the accident.

Molly Peterson was dead. It was too easy to blame the accident on someone who wasn't there to tell their side of the story or at least contribute to the facts. She just wished Molly were alive now to help clear things up for all of them.

Chapter Eight

Louise was full of questions for Teresa when she arrived at the café to get a cup of coffee and a donut before heading over to the clinic. Her sudden move and her part-time employment at the clinic, in particular, were hot topics of conversation. But as Dennis had informed her, the Stockington Falls Medical Clinic had several per diem staffers who only worked when needed, and this type of arrangement seemed to fit Teresa well while she was still taking time off from school. That seemed to satisfy Louise's curiosity.

The more she thought about it as she made her way across the street to the clinic, the more Teresa was glad she'd decided to work with the clinic, particularly on a part-time basis. The opportunity gave her a little spending money for what she needed, while not overloading herself with a full-time job in order to keep from draining her bank account until March when she could move back into her condo.

She said her hellos as she walked the hallway toward what was now going to be her office while she was in Stockington Falls. She'd meet with Benny there. Her heart raced with every step. Her first meeting with Benny had been in his room at the clinic. Yesterday's meeting had been in Dennis's office since her office was full of boxes. Today was the first day she'd been counseling in her own space. She passed right by Dennis's office and went into her own and sat down.

The office was empty. There were no pictures or little personal items that made it hers. But it would do. There were two comfortable chairs opposite the desk that would do nicely for her and Benny. It was a start.

She was surprised at how much more settled she felt here in her own office rather than in the other two arrangements. Having an office gave a sense of permanency to her stay here.

It didn't really matter. No matter how permanent it felt today, she was only going to be here a few months, so there was no sense making the place feel homey. Someone else would move in when she left. Until then, the office would do nicely for everyone involved.

Teresa pressed the button on the intercom, and Cammie answered.

"Need anything?"

"Can you please let me know when Benny is here?"

"Sure. And welcome."

Teresa smiled as she sat back. Hopefully everyone would still be feeling welcoming toward her at the end of today.

Dennis tried not to read anything into why Teresa just breezed by his office and into hers without even saying hello. She was probably nervous.

Guilt picked at him for pushing her so hard to help Benny. What if he'd gone too far? What if she really wasn't ready?

He'd prayed on it last night and wondered if the reason he'd pushed was as much for him as it was for Benny. He couldn't remember the last time he'd been as interested in a woman. Even his relationship with Donna had been slow to build. In the beginning, he'd thought that was a good thing. Slow and steady. He'd seen too many relationships burn out after starting strong. But their relationship had never fully won them over. They'd never truly committed themselves to each other, which, in the end, made it all too easy to let go.

From the moment he'd met Teresa, something

inside him had clicked. He liked having her around and felt like a teenage boy having the girl he has a crush on accept his invitation to the prom when Teresa agreed to stay in the guesthouse.

Ridiculous. He was a grown man. He was a doctor, after all. Men didn't have crushes. But he found his radar was up whenever Teresa Morales was near. Yet his feelings for her went beyond simple attraction. He also had enormous admiration for her work and for the commitment she showed to it—taking on Benny's case even when he could see that it scared her, just because she couldn't bring herself to abandon a child in need.

And though he did worry that he might have pushed her too hard, Dennis was glad he'd resolved Teresa's housing problems and found a way to keep her in town. Not just for him—but for Teresa, too. He still didn't know what had happened to her in Hartford, and he wouldn't search for answers without her permission, but he could tell it had wounded her deeply. He hoped that helping Benny would allow her to regain her confidence and overcome her past, but it called for a delicate balance. He didn't want to push her too hard or too fast and end up setting her up for another fall. Especially not now when he was coming to realize just how deeply, personally important it was to him to see her happy and whole once more.

"Who do you think you are?"

The deep voice from the man standing in the doorway of Dennis's office was familiar. He tried to defuse the angry tone with a greeting as he stood up from behind his desk.

"How are you doing, Frank? Are you here to pick up Benny?"

His brother-in-law scowled. "He's my son. Why wouldn't I?"

"Karen said you were working. That's why I offered to bring Benny home when he was done with his session with Ms. Morales."

Frank's face turned red with frustration. "John Peterson cancelled the week. I can't say I blame him, having to bury his wife and all. But it means no paycheck for the house. And before you go offering, I don't need your money. *We* don't need it."

"I wasn't going to offer. I know how you feel about that."

By all accounts, Frank was a proud man, with a strong sense of personal responsibility for his family. That wasn't a bad thing. But the pride he had could also be destructive when it meant his family suffered the consequences of his refusal to accept help. Still, Dennis treaded lightly.

"I know you'd tell me if there was anything I could do."

"Haven't you done enough damage already?"

Dennis suppressed a sigh. "Benny is in a lot of pain."

"And I'm his father. You go around talking to Karen and telling her he needs a shrink, and she's convinced she'll be a bad mother for not bringing him here. You think you're so smart. You always did. Big college degrees and big-time war hero."

Anger had Frank's face twisted into an ugly mask. There was so much pain behind it that Dennis couldn't help but wonder where it all came from. This wasn't the man he'd known all these years. He wasn't the same man Dennis had seen marry his sister and sit down at the dinner table at his parents' home so many times before.

Something had happened to his brother-in-law. Times were hard. But they'd been hard for everyone in Stockington Falls when the plant shut down. Hard times were no excuse for Frank's behavior.

"This isn't about me, Frank."

"Of course not. And like I said, Benny's not your kid. You don't have a right to butt in where it's none of your business."

"Karen is my sister, and Benny is my nephew. That makes it very much my business. And since I'm also Benny's physician, it's also my duty."

The sound of Teresa's footsteps coming down the hall cut into the argument. Frank's mouth twisted into a grim line as he pointed in the direction of where Teresa was coming from.

"She's just as bad. Big-city girl comes up to the small town to save the world. She has no right here."

"That's not why Teresa is here. But I'm glad she is."

"She'll leave. They all do. The sooner the better if you ask me."

The knock on the open door was expected. It was clear Teresa had heard the raised voices and concluded Frank's yelling was in part about her.

"Am I interrupting?" she asked, looking from Frank to Dennis.

"Yes," Frank said coldly.

"No," Dennis said at the same time. He didn't relish the idea of having Teresa assaulted by his brother-in-law's foul moods. But since she was counseling Benny, perhaps she knew how to convince Frank about the importance of Benny getting help.

Instead of being taken aback by the obvious tension in Dennis's office, Teresa smiled, no doubt in an effort to defuse tempers.

"Well, I'm glad we got that cleared up. Did you want to speak with me, Mr. Dulton?"

"How did you know who I am?"

"Benny showed me a picture of the two of you

fishing on Lake Champlain. It looked like the two of you were having a good time. He was a bit younger than he is now, but you haven't changed. Besides, he looks a lot like you."

Frank wasn't affected by the comparison to his son.

"Where's Benny?"

Teresa remained calm. "I sent him out to the truck. When I heard the two of you...talking I thought it was best."

Frank drew in a controlled breath. "I want you to leave my son alone."

"I understand your concern, Mr. Dulton. Your wife explained your feelings—"

"Obviously not enough for you to stay out of our lives."

"I can't do that."

"You can't mess up my kid's head without my permission."

She nodded and remained calm, which Dennis knew was probably infuriating Frank even more. He wanted a battle, and that was why he'd come to Dennis's office. He thought he'd get one there.

"You're right, Mr. Dulton," Teresa said. "But I only need one parent's permission, and I have your wife's. Unless you want to exercise your right to get a court order to stop me, I'll continue working with Benny. I certainly hope you don't do that though. Benny has a lot of problems."

Frank's eyebrows drew together. "What did he tell you?"

Teresa shook her head unapologetically. "That's confidential. I'm afraid I can't—"

"You told *her* though."

"Who? Are you talking about Karen?" Dennis asked.

"Yes." Darting his eyes from Dennis to Teresa, he added, "You probably told him what my son told you, too."

"No," Teresa said resolutely. "Unless he specifically talks about intent to harm himself, I can't disclose anything Benny tells me without his permission. He knows that because I've made that promise. And I *will* keep it."

"But he's a kid."

"He still has rights."

Teresa's face turned sympathetic. Dennis wondered just how many times she'd had to talk to worried parents about what their children had disclosed to her.

"Look, I know it feels odd not to have control over this. But I work with a lot of students. If they believed their every private thought was going to be broadcast, they'd never come to me in the first place. Kids need a place, a safe harbor of sorts, to vent and work through their feelings. It helps make them stronger and able to cope with the pressures of being a teenager."

"He can come to me. I'm his father."

"That's not always possible. Some kids—"

"You don't know my son!"

"No," she said. "But I want to know him."

Teresa had learned years ago how not to react when people came at her in anger. In the end, it was never about her. She knew that. It was about their own frustration that made them lash out at a convenient target. Frank Dulton was no different than Benny in that way. He was simply using her as a vehicle to express his anger.

Her usual response was to ask the Lord to give her strength to help ease the burden from the shoulders of the person who was obviously in pain. She did that again in silence.

"You people don't know anything at all. You come in here, and you think you can save the world. All my son needs is a little discipline. His mother spoils him too—"

Dennis interjected. "Frank, Benny tried to kill himself twice! That's not from spoiling or lack of discipline. You can't ignore that."

"Is that what Karen told you? He had some accidents is all. You're making a bigger deal out of it than it was."

Frank breezed by Teresa, making her quickly step into the office for fear he'd collide with her on his way to the door. Then he turned back to Dennis. "You couldn't even keep your own relationship with Donna together. I know. Karen told me all about how she packed up her stuff in the middle of the night and just left. You did nothing to try to get her back. And now you want to butt into my life and ruin my family by filling Karen's head with all this crazy stuff? Stay away from my family, Dennis. Things were fine when you weren't here. We don't need you here now."

"Whether you like it or not, Karen, Benny and even you, Frank, are my family. I'm not going anywhere."

With anger that could stop a rhino in its tracks, Frank Dulton swung around and stalked down the corridor of the clinic.

"Well, that went well," Dennis said, shaking his head. "I'm sorry you had to be subjected to that."

Taking a quick peek down the hallway, Teresa said as she closed his office door, "I can see there is no love lost between the two of you."

Dennis dragged his hand across his head. "It's probably hard to believe but it wasn't always like this. I actually got along really well with Frank when he first married Karen."

"Did you two have a falling out of some kind?"

"No. But time did change us all. Maybe being away is making me see things now that I wouldn't have seen if I'd been home all those years they'd been married. I can see now that I missed a lot of what was going on with my family when I was gone."

"How often were you home?"

"Weekend visits during college and during my residency, when I could spare the time. But I saw the most noticeable change when I got home from Iraq—in both Frank and my sister."

Teresa shrugged. "Maybe it wasn't there before. Things happen and people change. In this case, Benny was growing up. I'm sure his problems have become a problem for the entire family."

"It's not just Benny. Frank is different now. We got along, but we weren't particularly close as brothers-in-law. But I always knew Karen loved him, and I knew he worked hard to provide for the family."

"What changed that?"

"Losing his job when the plant closed changed things, but I don't know if Frank started acting differently right away. I wasn't here when it happened, and Karen doesn't say much. Then there was the fact that Karen had to go to work. That hit Frank hard. He's very old-fashioned that way. Needing the extra money after he got laid off was bad enough, but when Karen found work before he did, it probably made things worse. So he took the first job he could find. Good jobs are scarce in small towns, and unless your work has something to do with the ski resort, you have to take what you can get. In his case, it was construction work with Peterson's Construction."

"Sometimes losing a job is all it takes to make a marriage unravel. Not that I'm saying that's where they're headed. I don't know them."

"Karen's different, too. More timid. Like I said, she doesn't say much. But she's not as happy as she once was. I can tell."

"Have you really talked to her about it? I mean, asked her directly if there is something going on at home? It's not like you're a stranger. You're her brother."

He shrugged. "I pray on that all the time. Where is my boundary? I mean, yes, she's my sister and I love her. But do I really have the right to meddle in her personal relationship with her husband?" He sat down at his desk and fiddled with a pencil. "It's crazy. I find myself looking for bruises, other signs that maybe Karen is in trouble. I hate that I do that. So far I have never seen anything. But I wonder if I really don't want to see it, too. It's sometimes easier to see what's going on when it's a stranger instead of the people you love."

A flicker of pain stabbed at Teresa, and then it was gone. "You're right. Sometimes you can be too close to a situation to see things clearly."

"Do you have any more sessions this afternoon?"

"No, I'm done."

"Are you going to be sticking around the clinic for a while or heading back to the guesthouse to air it out? Or is it no longer standing?"

Her lips pulled into a crooked grin. "It's fine. How'd you find out? I wanted to tell you myself."

"Carlos called me right after he left. Told me I needed to give you some woodstove 101 lessons."

She laughed. "And here I was planning to take you out to lunch to butter you up so I could tell you about it. That is, if you can get away."

His face split into a grin that erased the worried lines that were there earlier. "That sounds like a good plan. It's slow here today. And after my run-in with Frank, I could use some air. I'm sure Cammie can hold down the fort. And I know just the place we can go."

Chapter Nine

Vermont was filled with little hole-in-the-wall diners as well as quaint restaurants that were part of bed-and-breakfasts tucked away on quiet country roads. If you weren't paying attention, it was easy to miss them. Dennis suggested one such place near the river in the next town.

He pulled his SUV up into the small parking lot and killed the engine.

Teresa pulled her jacket tighter against her chest to ward off the cold wind that had picked up since this morning. The smell of snow to come hung heavy in the air.

"They have the best homemade bread here. I hope you're not in a hurry, though. Roma cooks everything to order."

"I have no plans. But aren't you needed back at the clinic?"

"Slow day. As long as no one gets hurt skiing on the mountain today, Cammie won't need me."

"Then let's hope for careful skiing and snow-boarding."

"Yes."

Like the gentleman he was, Dennis opened the restaurant door and allowed Teresa to walk in before him. The foyer was decorated with fine period antiques and a large oriental style rug. The heavy desk sitting in the center of the large foyer had a guest book and a stack of pamphlets that highlighted tourist attractions in Vermont. Next to the pamphlets was a stack of menus.

When the face of the elderly woman seated behind the desk lit up with recognition, Dennis returned the smile and showed two fingers.

"Well, I don't often get to see you for lunch, Dennis. If I'd known you were coming, I would have put the pot roast in the oven a bit earlier so you could take some home for dinner."

"That's okay, Roma. Much as I love your pot roast, I'm going to stick with something a little quicker on the menu."

"Things are busy at the clinic, I take it? I heard about that terrible accident a few days ago. Terrible shame. Just terrible."

"Yes, it was."

The woman turned to Teresa. "My name is Roma. It's so nice of you to join us here."

Teresa grasped the woman's outstretched hand and gave it a gentle squeeze. "It's a pleasure to meet you, Roma. I'm Teresa."

"Did you just move to the area, or are you vacationing?"

The question, while innocent, stumped Teresa, and she didn't exactly know how to answer. She'd stayed longer than most people who vacationed in Stockington Falls. She had no plans to leave yet, but that didn't mean she was a permanent resident by any means.

"I'm new to the area," she finally answered.

"I'm sure you're going to love it here. If you're both in a hurry, I do have a few things on the menu that I can whip up quick. Why don't you both come with me? We have a fire burning nicely in the dining room. I'll get you a warm loaf of maple bread to start with while you look at the menu."

Teresa quickly glanced at Dennis, who mouthed, "The most fabulous bread in the world."

She chuckled softly as she followed the elderly woman into the next room. There were no more than five small tables in the dining room. Roma seated the two of them at the table closest to the commanding stone fireplace that was large enough for a person to stand inside. The stonework covered the entire back wall. The fire was inviting and did wonders to dispel the chill she'd felt from the wind outside.

Teresa removed her jacket, hooking it on to one of the hooks nailed to the wall where two other ski parkas were already hanging. Dennis did the same. As she sat down, Teresa rubbed her hands together against the heat radiating from the fire.

"This beats the Twin Falls Café for charm," she said.

"Roma is a terrific cook, too. I wasn't kidding about the bread. She makes this maple bread to die for."

"I take it you like to come here often."

He shrugged. "A couple of times a month. I'd come here more, but the café's so much more convenient when I'm at the clinic. I like to come here when I can, though. It's home cooking that I don't get by myself."

"Or not at all, since you don't cook that often.

"Exactly."

"I have to say though that you didn't do too bad with the chicken fajitas the other night."

His slight grin showed he was pleased at her compliment. "They would have made Cammie proud."

She chuckled and looked at the menu. After they ordered, they settled in with sliced maple bread and warm apple cider. The fire felt soothing and brought thoughts of curling up in an overstuffed sofa with a good book. But Teresa enjoyed the company she was in right now. It made it hard for her to broach the subject she knew was not going to be pleasant.

"Frank Dulton was pretty upset earlier," Teresa said.

Dennis nodded, his large hands wrapped loosely around his stoneware mug.

"Something tells me it's more than just me seeing Benny for counseling that set him off."

"You mean his animosity toward me." Dennis said the words more of a conclusion than a question.

She tried to be as delicate as possible. "It's hard to ignore…from both of you."

Dennis shrugged with a slow sigh.

"I never said I was perfect."

"I don't expect you to be."

Dennis leaned back in his chair and looked around the small dining room, avoiding her gaze. But only for a moment.

"I told you earlier that Frank and I weren't always like this. But something changed. Things have been hard on them. Frank didn't grow up in a family where people talked about their feelings where Karen is just the opposite."

It was beginning to make sense. "That's why it's hard for him to understand why Benny needs some professional help?"

"Right. Only I've suspected that it goes deeper than that. Things have been difficult for them financially. As you saw, Frank is a proud man. I can understand his pride making it hard for him to talk to outsiders about his situation, but he doesn't really talk to Karen, either."

"Did she confide in you?"

"A little. And only after I press. We've always had a good relationship, but I've long suspected since I came back from Iraq that Frank wasn't happy that I returned. He didn't mind our relationship being so close when I was in med school or during my residency I suspect because I wasn't around. But when I came back—"

"You were in his face."

He shrugged. "Or so he perceived. My sister was thrilled to have me back, but I didn't receive the same warm reception from Frank. I got the feeling he liked it better when I was somewhere else and only called or wrote occasionally."

"Maybe it made it easier to pretend that things were okay."

"You mean easier to hide. Karen only told me about Benny's depression when I came home."

"That must have been quite a shock for you."

"Yes, and one filled with some measure of guilt. I feel like I should have been here. Pastor Balinski had been seeing Karen in church and counseling the family, but slowly Benny stopped attending services with her. Frank, not at all."

Teresa thought about it a moment. "Do you think it's jealousy?"

"With Frank? Could be. But I've long believed Frank had his own issues that needed to be dealt with. He just gets angry if Karen brings it up."

"I'm sorry things are so difficult with your family. Family issues can bring such stress. For what it's worth, Frank really needs you to step in and be strong where he can't be. I'm sure he'd hate that I said that, but after that display in your office, I'm sure there is more fear and frustration driving him than anger."

Roma returned to the table before long and delivered their meals. As Dennis said it would be, the meal was cooked to perfection and was nothing like anything Teresa had eaten in a while. Because of time, they skipped coffee and headed back to the clinic.

There were several cars in the parking lot when they climbed out of Dennis's SUV. Dennis pulled his cell phone out of his jacket pocket and checked for messages. "It can't be too bad. No one called me in from lunch early."

"Do you think Cammie is back from lunch?"

"Her car is here. She's probably just getting in."

"Good."

Dennis held Teresa back with his hand. "Now may not be the best time to talk with her."

"Why?"

"They made the preparation for Molly's funeral this morning. I'm going to go out on a limb and say she's probably not up to doing much talking this afternoon."

"Oh, you're right. Perhaps another day when she's had some time. Besides, I think it can wait."

Teresa pulled her car keys out of her purse and turned to walk over to her car.

"You're not coming in?" Dennis asked.

"No, I'm done for the day, and I have an important errand."

His eyebrows drew together. "What do you have, a hot date?"

She chuckled teasingly. "Yeah, with the chief of police."

She left Dennis standing there with his mouth open. She climbed into her sedan and fired the engine as she watched him shake his head and walk into the clinic. She liked teasing Dennis. He could be so serious about his work and the things he was passionate about. But there was a playful side of him that she enjoyed.

* * *

"I'm afraid there isn't much here that we didn't already know," Mac said, handing Teresa the police report he'd just received from the state police.

Teresa sighed. She was hoping—for what, she didn't really know. She handed the report back to Mac.

"Sorry it wasn't more help to you," he said.

"Me, too. But I appreciate the help."

"Do you mind my asking what exactly you were hoping to find?"

Teresa leaned back in the chair. "I guess a time-line. Benny is feeling an enormous amount of guilt. It's not uncommon after an accident but strange in that he's taken on the burden for the entire accident as if he caused it. Yet, he said that he saw Molly's Bronco already in the water when he drove into the bridge."

"There was a gaping hole left in the side of the bridge after the Bronco tore through it. Molly must have been driving fast or have gone into quite a spin to break through that way."

Teresa thought a moment. "Was there any damage on the other side of the bridge? I mean, if she did spin, you'd think she would have careened against the rail on the other side."

Mac looked at the report and then pulled out another file with notes written on it. "The highway department only noted fixing one side of the bridge."

"That doesn't mean there aren't markings."

"True. But I still don't know how it would matter to Benny."

Teresa leaned back in the chair and let a slow breath escape her lips. "I'm grasping at straws. I'm looking for an answer that points definitively to a reason for what he's feeling, and there may not be one here at all."

She looked up at Mac, who now seemed somewhere else. "Will you be going to Molly's funeral?"

He looked at her then, his eyes sad. Then he nodded. "She was a friend."

"I'm sorry for your loss."

"Me, too. Will you be there?"

She hadn't thought about going, but now that Mac had broached the subject Teresa decided she may consider it. But would it be too awkward?

"I'm not sure. I never knew Molly, and I don't want to be the out-of-towner who crashed the party." She kept to herself her fears that it might be too emotionally draining for her, her first funeral since Mariah's.

He nodded. "There's no hope for either of us on that front. I just wondered, um, if you need anything else, just let me know."

"There may be one thing." Teresa thought a minute. "Do you mind doing a little experiment with me?"

Mac sat down on the edge of his desk. "What type of experiment?"

"I'd like to take this report and go out to the bridge myself so I can walk through the steps of the accident."

"What would that prove?"

"I don't know." She sighed. "Like I said, I know I'm grasping at straws. I just feel like I'm missing something." She released a sigh full of frustration. "Maybe I'm losing a battle that I never had a hope of winning."

Mac smiled then. "There's always hope."

Teresa had thought that at one time, too. As she left Mac to his work and drove the distance back to Dennis's place, she wondered if figuring this out would get her any closer to feeling that way again.

Chapter Ten

"Aren't you done grilling me yet?"

Benny stared at Teresa with the typical boredom of a seventeen-year-old who wanted to be anywhere other than where he was. It had been a week since the accident and a few days since Molly Peterson's funeral. Now that the teenagers were back at school, Teresa wanted to know how Benny was handling the pressure.

From his reaction to her question, she guessed it wasn't going well.

This past hour with Benny had Teresa's head throbbing. Although they'd made progress and Benny wasn't just staring at her through the whole hour, what he did contribute to the session left her with more questions than clarity. She could only imagine how he felt.

One thing was clear: the root of Benny's problems didn't lie with the New Year's Eve accident.

Sure, it certainly contributed to his current state of mind, which at best would be deemed by any professional as shaky. But there were other problems he'd been battling long before that night.

She tried to focus on the positive.

"I spoke with Chuck's mother this morning. His condition has been upgraded from critical to serious."

There was a flicker of interest in Benny's dark eyes. Still he kept his slumped-back position in the chair. "Is there a difference?"

"Absolutely. I don't want to lie to you. He's got a long road ahead of him. But his mom was told his condition has improved. He's a strong kid."

The news should have come as a relief to Benny, and she'd expected at least a little reaction. A smile. A mutter of thanks. But he just stared out the window.

"You don't believe me?"

Benny shrugged. "He's still in a coma, right?"

"Yes. But it's a drug-induced coma now."

"What does that mean?"

"It means his doctor has given him medication to keep him comfortable so he can heal. When he improves a little more, they'll stop giving him the medication and he should wake up just fine."

It was clear that to Benny there was no difference at all, and he wasn't pleased. Where she had felt encouraged by the news she'd received earlier this morning, Benny sighed and slumped his shoulders. As long as Chuck remained lost in a coma, unable to talk, Benny wouldn't see his friend's progress as any progress at all.

"I'm not trying to bowl you over, Benny. I just want to help—"

She was rewarded with an exasperated sigh and a roll of his eyes. Nothing she hadn't seen before. "I don't need a shrink."

She'd heard this type of reproach before and quickly countered it. "Shrinks are psychiatrists, and I'm not a psychiatrist. I'm a child psychologist."

"So?"

"There's a difference."

"I thought you said you were a doctor."

"I didn't go to school quite as long as your uncle did, but I do have a Ph.D. in child psychology. Your uncle did his time in med school, not me."

He stared at her skeptically for a brief moment. "Well, it's all the same to me if you're trying to get into my head. Ain't gonna change things one way or the other, you know. You're wasting your time."

"I'll be the judge of that. But why don't you enlighten me. Why is this a waste of time?"

He slouched back in the chair, shoulders drooping, and legs spread wide, one boot furiously connecting with the leg of her desk as he repeatedly kicked it in short little bursts. Each motion jarred her, but she kept herself from flinching.

"Look around you," he said. "You haven't been here long, so you still like Stockington Falls. But if you stick around long enough, you won't anymore."

"You don't like it here?"

"Nothing good ever happens here. My father lived his whole life in the house we still live in. He never goes anywhere or does anything but work and come home and yell at my mother. It's like a prison there. And I'll be in that prison or another one long after you drive out of this nothing town."

"Prison? That's a strong choice of words." Did he worry that he'd be charged with a crime for the accident?

Another roll of the eyes. "Behind bars or stuck in Stockington Falls. It's all the same, ain't it? It's just another prison."

"Isn't there anything you like about Stockington Falls?"

"What's to like? You think I want to end up like these folks here? People come from out of town to bum on the slopes, and they just look at us like we're freaks or something. I don't want to end up working in some dead-end job at Peterson's

Construction like my old man because that's the only thing he could get. And I don't want to have to pick up after tourists either. I don't know why my uncle ever came back here. He was free. He saw something better than this hick town. Here there's nothing but people passing through."

Teresa picked up a dull pointed pencil and tapped it on her blank notepad. She liked that Benny was talking even if she didn't like what he was saying. Maybe she had a chance to change things to the positive.

"You told me before that you've decided not to go to college."

"So?"

"You say you don't like it here. Have you ever thought about college as a way to get out?"

She knew he had. Dennis had told her as much. But about a year ago, he'd stopped talking about colleges, ignoring his uncle any time Dennis brought the subject up. She wanted to hear it from Benny's mouth why he'd had a change of heart.

"Why bother? My folks don't have money for college. 'Sides, my dad doesn't think I'm worth much as it is."

Teresa's insides burned with fury, but she squashed it down. At a time when kids needed encouragement, it was hard to stomach anyone who'd run them down or take away their dreams.

She could see by the look on Benny's face that Dennis had been right. Benny *did* want to go to college, if only to get away from Stockington Falls and what he thought was holding him back.

Whether it was Stockington Falls or the city of Hartford, it didn't matter. Kids Benny's age wanted to spread their wings and see what the world had to offer. She had a feeling Benny had a better chance of doing that with his mother's help. But first, he needed to get over this idea—which he seemed to have gotten from his father—that he couldn't do it.

Teresa suppressed a sigh and pinched the bridge of her nose before going on. This could very well be the root of Benny's troubles. Emotional abuse was just as painful as a closed-fisted punch to the face, just as destructive. But it was easier to cover up the bruising until something tragic happened.

Benny was bruised all over.

In all thy ways acknowledge Him and He shall direct thy path.

Dennis said that Benny had stopped going to church services with Karen. It wasn't uncommon. Many teenagers strayed from their faith, thinking they didn't need the Lord in their lives. Those same teenagers come back to God when they are ready. But Teresa couldn't help but think that if only Benny embraced his faith again, he'd find the direction and comfort he needed in his life right now.

She leaned forward in her seat, resting her elbows on her knees, eyeing Benny. "For a minute, let's forget about what your father thinks. If you did go to college, what would you do?"

A small glint of light flashed in the corner of Benny's eyes, but his face changed instantly and grew hard, the ray of hope Teresa snatched vanishing. He wanted to go there. She could tell. But he was afraid.

She wouldn't push it. She'd wait until he was ready to talk more about it.

"Well, I won't be driving a truck for a living."

"Why's that?"

"Come on, doc. I've told you the story of what happened on the bridge a ton of times. I'm nothing but a lousy driver. I saw the hole in the bridge and the car in the water. I panicked, and then I slid off the road and hit the tree on the other side. End of story. I can't do anything right."

He went silent, closing himself off.

"Things were pretty crazy New Year's Eve, Benny. Maybe you remember something else that could—"

"They want to pin the accident on me." Benny unleashed the words with raw emotion. "Don't you think I hear what people are saying? They all say it was my fault and I was partying, but they're wrong. I wasn't drunk. I wasn't. No matter what my ol' man says. I wasn't drunk."

Benny bolted up in his seat. His eyes were frightfully wide, reminding Teresa of a rabbit checkmated by a fox.

"It was the stupid truck plowing right over the bridge coming toward me. It didn't even have its lights on. What was I supposed to do? Stupid truck caused the accident and I couldn't— And now that lady's dead and Chuck's going to die, too, and it's because of me."

"I told you Chuck is doing much better. It's just a matter of time before he comes out of the coma," she said sympathetically.

No matter what words of wisdom she offered him—no matter what anyone said—Benny couldn't be consoled.

"I think maybe it's time to take a trip to St. Johnsbury," she said.

"What for?"

"To see Chuck. I think it's important to see for yourself that he is doing better. How about I talk to your mother about it?"

"We only have the one car. Dad needs it for work."

"Then maybe your uncle will take you. I'm sure

he wouldn't mind if you asked him. In fact, he'd probably like to spend the time with you."

Benny's voice hitched. His bottom lip was in a thin, tight line as he held on to the last fragments of his control. "It should have been me."

"But it wasn't you."

"Yeah, well, it should've been. I wish I'd done it sooner. None of this would have happened. Chuck would be okay and…none of it!" Benny stopped his tirade, clenching every muscle in his face, holding back a tidal wave of emotion.

Abruptly, he charged from the chair and sped through the door like crumpled leaves on a gust of winter wind. Although Teresa was on his heels, Benny was already halfway down the hall and racing toward the clinic door. Karen Dulton, who had been waiting in the lobby, snapped a startled glance back at Teresa, then raced out the door after her son.

Dennis strode out of his office just in time to see the whole show. As he rushed by her, Teresa put out her arm to stop him. "Let Karen do it," she said.

"No luck?" he asked.

Teresa dragged some much-needed air into her lungs. Her pulse was pounding from the adrenaline rush of Benny's tirade. "Actually, yes. Getting to the heart of what gives pain is never easy, Dennis.

It's going to take him some time, but I think I chipped away a little at that shell he's been hiding under."

Dennis glanced down, his gaze settling on her hand on his arm. Her eyes followed until she saw what had captured Dennis's attention. Her hand was visibly trembling. She reached up and clamped her arms around her middle in an effort to steady herself.

"I'm okay."

"Are you sure?"

"Yes, Dennis. I'm fine. It's just—"

"Come here," Dennis said, opening his arms to her.

She lifted her chin resolutely. "No."

She couldn't have him hold her. Not like this. She wasn't the one who needed comfort here. Benny was. She just wished that every time she saw Benny her mind didn't wander back to that autumn day at Mariah's house.

News of David's death in the car accident just days before had shocked all of them, especially Mariah.

More shocking was that David's accident had happened just after he'd had a fight with Mariah. She'd told him she was pregnant and he'd said that he didn't want the baby, fearing he'd have to change his college plans or lose his football scholarship.

After the fight, he was driving fast and careless, not reacting to the black ice in time. Since they held the fight accountable for David's recklessness, many of his teammates and friends blamed Mariah for his death.

David hadn't been there to defend her when raw feelings turned ugly. Grief counselors, including Teresa, had focused on the loss, not the aftermath of anger the classmates had felt toward Mariah, leaving Mariah to take the brunt of it alone, until it all became too much for her and suicide seemed like the only way out.

Thinking about it made Teresa want to run away again, but Dennis ignored her plea and drew her tightly into the circle of his arms right there in the middle of the hallway. In her mind, Teresa told herself it was completely unprofessional—for both of them. But she found herself sinking against his broad chest, absorbing all the warmth and comfort he offered. She loved that he was unabashedly open about his feelings and his concern. She'd seen that from the first and had been drawn to it, drawn to the man.

"I need your help," she murmured, her head against his chest.

He bent his head and lightly kissed her forehead. "You got me any way you want me, lady."

Chapter Eleven

Call it ego, but when Teresa had asked for his help, the last thing he'd expected was to go traipsing through a thigh-high snowbank on the banks of Abbey Bridge. The striking image of its barn-red color siding glowing like neon against the white snow blanketing the ground hardly made up for being stuck outside in the bitter cold.

"What are we looking for?" he asked Teresa as she paced up and down between the span of the bridge.

She stopped in front of him and propped her fists on her hips. "I haven't a clue. I guess I hoped that by coming down here and seeing for myself how everything played out New Year's Eve that I could understand why Benny feels so responsible. I mean, it's normal for him to feel bad, even if it isn't his fault. He was driving. But this is deeper."

"Maybe it doesn't have anything to do with the

accident at all," Dennis said. "Maybe it's everything else going on in his life that he's upset about."

"Could be. But if that's the case, why does he keep mentioning the accident? He's the one who's bringing it up lately. Not me."

Dennis peered over the boarded-over railing where Molly's car had skidded on the slippery road before meeting its end. Layers of fresh snow covered the once-glaring scars from the accident that had claimed the young mother's life several weeks ago. Except for the simple wood beams used to patch the inside of the bridge, there was no evidence that an accident occurred here.

Dennis glanced up at the sound of an approaching car.

"Oh, good. I asked Dan MacKenzie to stop by, too."

"What do you think Mac can tell you that wasn't in the report?"

"I don't know."

Teresa shook her head and sighed, a cloud of mist emitting from her mouth. She looked adorably frustrated, and he found himself wishing he could kiss her anxiety away.

She'd probably punch him if he tried, he mused with a smile. She didn't seem like the type to stand for any distractions when she was on a fact-finding mission.

Just as well, he reminded himself. She wasn't planning to stay, so he shouldn't do anything to make himself fall for her even harder. It'd just make it more difficult to let her go.

It was a relief to see Mac's car approach. Dennis liked Mac, though he knew that the welcome to Stockington Falls that the Memphis native had received could be considered lukewarm at best. But he was a determined man, and Stockington Falls needed someone who was committed to sticking with the job.

Dennis guessed Mac to be about a few years younger than his thirty-five years, maybe a little less. But not by much. Not used to dealing with the staunch letter of the law, the townspeople balked when some of the minor infractions that living in a remote area allowed were no longer viewed in a lax manner. Dan MacKenzie was heavy-handed about crime of all kinds. The occasional request for a fixed traffic ticket fell on deaf ears.

But Dennis couldn't help but approve of how Mac absolutely adored Cammie Reynolds. Despite them being polar opposites on some extremes, he and Cammie walked the same line on what mattered most in life. Dennis always wondered what it was that ended a relationship that seemed so perfect from the start.

Mac tipped his hat to Teresa as he ambled up the

slight incline toward the bridge. "Good afternoon, ma'am."

"I know you're probably sick of hearing from me, Dan, but thank you for indulging me once again. I hope it wasn't too much trouble."

"It's a slow day."

"I promise this will be the last time."

"What seemed to be the problem?" Mac said in his deep Southern drawl.

"No problem," Teresa said, digging her hands deep into the pocket of her peacoat. "I was just wondering if you could walk me through the chain of events the state police came up with for what happened here New Year's Eve."

Mac gripped the wide rim of his police hat, adjusting it on his head. "I thought it pretty much stated things the way they were in that report I showed you, Teresa. From what I got from Ms. Pryor, the operator of the Trooper, Molly Peterson's Bronco was traveling southbound toward Abbey Bridge. Ms. Pryor was headed up to the lodge when she saw headlights on the wrong side of the road."

"I thought Allie Pryor lived on the other side of town," Dennis said. "Why would she be heading back up the mountain at that hour of the evening? It was almost midnight."

"Vanessa told me all the staff were asked to attend the gala," Teresa told him.

Mac nodded. "I confirmed that when I talked to the staff. And Allie hadn't been feeling well earlier and came late."

Teresa pointed to the long and winding road heading away from the ski resort. "Benny was coming down the mountain, just a little ways after Molly."

"Yes, ma'am."

"What would Benny be doing up on the mountain? I didn't see him at the resort party," Dennis said. "But the event was huge. He could have been anywhere."

"Chuck's mother told me Chuck had a job at the resort ski shop," Teresa added. "His shift was over, and he didn't want to wait for his parents to pick him up so he called Benny to come get him."

"I'm afraid the young kids like to have fun on some of the fire roads leading into the hills," Mac said. "It was bad weather to be doing that. Of course, once Gary Estabrooks sells off that land next to the resort to the Kaufmanns, that'll end. The whole landscape of the mountain will change if they end up expanding the ski resort like they plan. Either that or I'm going to have to get used to camping out at the end of the fire road just to keep them off the mountain."

Teresa glanced around at the stand of pine trees at the mouth of the seventy-five-foot covered bridge. She walked over and touched the angry spot where metal had connected with the tree. "Benny hit here and Allie Pryor—"

"The opposite side, right along that stone wall there," Mac said.

"And what about Molly Peterson's Bronco?"

Again, Mac pointed to the mountain road leading from the resort. "From what I gather, she'd been at the gala and was heading home toward the bridge."

"I saw her briefly," Dennis said. "She and Drew were there for about twenty minutes, and then I don't remember seeing them again."

Teresa stared at the snow-covered scenery as she nibbled on her thumbnail. "Benny insists there was a truck going too fast. No headlights, he said."

"No one should be going fast on this bridge when they're the only vehicle. Never mind bad weather and multiple cars," Mac said.

Mac glanced at Dennis, then back at Teresa. "I don't know. There's no mention in the report about a car or truck with no headlights on. Why would they be coming through the bridge with no headlights?"

Dennis agreed. "It's a recipe for disaster."

"They converged on this area all within a few

seconds of each other," Teresa continued. "Molly was headed down the hill in the same direction that Benny was going. Allie was coming up but never made it through the bridge. Benny said he saw the hole in the bridge before he noticed Molly's car in the water."

"I was under the assumption that the Bronco exploded when it went into the water," Mac said, adjusting his hat. "If the hole was already there, and Molly's car had already gone over, then he should have seen the fire first, especially with that gaping hole in the wall of the bridge opening up the view."

"You think Benny is confused?" Dennis asked. "He didn't have enough alcohol in his system for him to have been confused as a result of that, but he is an inexperienced driver. And with the bad road conditions on New Year's Eve, well, he could have hit a patch, got spun around and didn't know how to recover."

Teresa looked around. "That's enough to shake up anyone. It may have taken him a while to notice the Bronco was on fire. Even an experienced driver can get disoriented."

Mac sighed. "My best guess is that Benny lost control when he got distracted by the sight of the hole. He swerved, setting off Allie's accident. Simple as that. If there was another truck, it was long gone by the time the emergency service came on the scene."

"You think it was Allie's Trooper coming up that Benny's thinking of?" Teresa went over to the marks on the inside of the bridge where Molly's Bronco busted through the wall. "He sees the big hole in the side of the bridge and gets nervous. When people see things out of the ordinary, they stare."

"Maybe he saw the Trooper at the last second, and it made him swerve again as he came out of the bridge, causing him to hit the tree," Dennis said.

"I have to admit, after reviewing the state police's reconstruction of the accident there does seem to be some holes in this investigation that need filling."

"For instance?" Dennis said.

Mac stood tall with his hands propped on his hips, his legs slightly parted. "Benny should have seen the explosion as he rounded the corner to Abbey Road. But he said he was already out of his car when it happened."

"That's right," Teresa added. "He thought it was fireworks going off at first. But he had hit his head on the steering wheel, so who knows if he was even coherent enough to know what happened."

"He was," Dennis said. Dazed, confused and

already full of remorse, Benny had immediately retreated into an inner world to find comfort, he recalled, but not showing any signs of decreased cognition. "His head injury wasn't the reason we kept him overnight."

"So you're saying you think Benny may be right and the Bronco didn't explode right away?" Teresa asked.

"It could be. I just don't know. For now, the report shows exactly what the state police came up with when they reconstructed the scene."

"But none of that answers my question," Teresa said. "Benny didn't cause Molly Peterson's Bronco to go into the river. By his own admission, the accident had already happened by the time he got here. It may have only been seconds before, but at least he can be sure his driving wasn't what caused Molly's death. So why does he seem to feel responsible for Molly's death?"

"You think that's what he's been upset about all this time?" Dennis asked. "I thought he was worried about Chuck."

"He still is. I'm sure that's definitely part of it. But one detail at a time, please."

"So where's the hole in the report?" Dennis asked.

Mac motioned for them all to walk over to the edge of the bridge. Dennis and Teresa followed.

Pointing to the opposite bank, Mac said, "There's one thing that has been bugging me for a while. Something I just can't wrap my mind around."

"What's that?" Dennis said.

Again, Mac pointed to the bank of the river flowing under Abbey Bridge and then to a spot directly beneath the hole in the bridge where the Bronco had busted through the rail.

"Look at the distance between the hole in the bridge and the riverbank where Drew was found."

"What about it?" Teresa asked.

"Drew Peterson is seven years old and about yay tall." Mac put his hand out as if measuring an imaginary child. "If my memory serves me right, his clothes weren't all that wet when he was put into the ambulance, were they? The fire chief who was first on the scene said he was thrilled to find Drew in such a good state, physically. His clothes were virtually dry, not indicative of being submersed in water."

Teresa glanced at the distance again. "But that's impossible. He's so small. He would have had to swim to get to shore, unless the blast blew him there, in which case he'd have landed harder and ended up with much more injuries."

"Or unless someone carried him out of the car," Dennis said.

"Are you sure about this?" Teresa asked.

Dennis thought long and hard about that night. "There was so much going on that night, and there was a lag in the time between when Drew was admitted to emergency and when I attended to him. I was with Chuck a long while before he was airlifted to St. Johnsbury. By the time I got to Drew, he was dressed in a hospital gown. Cammie took care of that. I know his injuries were too minor to indicate that he'd been carried by the blast, but I'm less sure about the swimming. I can't be sure if Drew's clothes were dry or not until I read Cammie's report."

Mac sighed. "Neither can I, and it's been nagging at me. We've been assuming the boy somehow climbed out of the vehicle, but take a look here."

Teresa and Dennis followed Mac to the side of the road, stopping at the railing leading to the side of the bridge where Drew was found. The water rushed wildly under the bridge.

Teresa gasped. "There is no way a small child could swim easily against the flow of that water."

"You're right," Dennis said. He couldn't imagine how Drew even survived the crash, let alone managed to escape the vehicle before it exploded. God was with him for sure.

Mac pointed to the spot where the Bronco plunged into the water. "The boy was seated in the backseat. Even if he jumped a good distance from where he was sitting, he would have landed in the water. The back door was open. But it could have blown open during the explosion or when the Bronco fell headfirst into the water."

Dennis shook his head in amazement. "Either way, if Drew got out of that car on his own, he would have certainly soaked his clothes through and been hypothermic by the time Carlos and the EMTs arrived on the scene. I would have remembered that. We would have been more worried about hypothermia."

Teresa crossed her arms across her chest. "There's something else that is bothering me about this, too."

"What's that?"

"Drew is so young. It's strange a child that young would leave his mother in the car. Children don't often leave their parents when they are frightened. It would make more sense for a child his age to stay by his mother's side and wait for help."

Dennis thought back to the distant look on Drew's face. Seeing a car explode with someone you love still inside was enough to send anyone over the edge. But for a child...

"Drew must not have been belted in the backseat.

He had to have been thrown from the Bronco when it started to spin, before the explosion. By the grace of God, he ended up on the bank instead of in the water," Mac concluded.

"For him, I'd say that was a blessing," Dennis added.

"But we'll never know for sure because the boy's not talking much about it. It may take a long time before he does." Mac turned to Teresa. "Has he said anything to you?"

Teresa shook her head. "Nothing. Although, I haven't had much chance to talk with him. John Peterson said Drew is understandably having a rough time and that he's blocked out most of what happened that night. He doesn't want to grill Drew about what happened to his mother."

Mac gave a heavy sigh. "Then I think that's about as close to a clear picture of what happened here New Year's Eve as anyone is going to get."

Dennis looked at Teresa's face. Disappointment clouded her expression. She'd clearly wanted some answers, and today's trek to the bridge hadn't provided any. It had only brought on more questions.

For Dennis, it had brought home something far more important. He didn't want to see anyone die. But the circumstances being what they were it could have easily been far worse for Benny, Karen and Frank if Benny's car had slid just a few feet over and ended up in the water as Molly's Bronco had. Dennis closed his eyes at the thought. His sister was so fragile right now. He couldn't imagine how she would have survived losing her son completely.

As if sensing his distress, Teresa placed a gentle hand on his arm. That one small move did wonders to dispel the anxiety building up inside him over what could have been. Right now Teresa could be a comfort to him and he'd take whatever comfort he could get. He only hoped he wouldn't feel an empty hole in his heart when she finally left Stockington Falls. It made him determined to find a way to make her stay.

Chapter Twelve

"How's the smell in the cottage?"

As she walked by one of the rooms, Teresa turned and saw Carlos standing by the nurses' station, chuckling.

"It's almost gone," Teresa said with a smile. "I have to say that I'm going to miss that woodsy smell when I leave here."

"Oh, don't tell me you're leaving us already," Carlos said.

Cammie, who was seated at the nurses' station, looked up from her paperwork but said nothing.

Teresa's shoulder's drooped. "This was only a temporary situation for me. But don't worry, I'll still be around for another month. Stockington Falls won't get rid of me that easy."

"If I had my way, you wouldn't be leaving at all," Dennis said, coming up to the nurses' station with Allie Pryor in tow. He dwarfed her as she sat in the wheelchair.

"I see your ride is here to pick you up," he said to Allie.

"Yes, thanks, Dr. Harrington. My brother is going to be at my house in a few hours, so Carlos and his wife will watch over me until then."

"Good. Let me know if you experience any unusual pain."

"You mean other than Carlos and my brother's ribbing?"

Carlos made a comical face. "You secretly love me."

"I don't know how Brenda puts up with you," she said, laughing.

"It's my Latin charm. Speaking of Brenda, she's making your favorite stew. Remind me to pick up some bread on the way home."

Teresa smiled and turned to Allie. "You take care, and if you need anything or just want to talk, please call me."

"I will. Thank you, Teresa."

Teresa walked out of the room and down the hall toward her office. *Her office.* With every step she took, it gave her a sense that permanency was cementing her feet in Stockington Falls. She couldn't deny that the people of the community had managed to wrap themselves around her heart. One person in particular.

She sighed as she walked into her office and closed the door. As she sat down at her desk, bare from all the little knickknacks and pictures she had in her office at the school in Hartford, she tried to remember how many of the neighbors she knew in her condo back home. Not many. Mrs. Dowling across the hall was someone she exchanged pleasantries with on occasion when they happened to be coming or going at the same time. She knew faces of the people who lived on the first floor, but none of their names.

It seemed odd to her now that she knew so many people in Stockington Falls after such a short period of time when she knew very few in the very building she'd lived in for four years.

Dragging a deep breath of air into her lungs, she suddenly felt claustrophobic. She needed to get out so she grabbed her purse and her jacket. After closing her office door, she walked the length of the hall to the front door. What stopped her escape completely was Cammie.

"Dennis said you wanted to talk to me, Teresa," Cammie said as she started to walk by.

"Ah, yes. Yes, I do."

She looked back at the office door she'd just locked securely.

"Would right now work for you? I just need to take her out to the car and then I can meet with you."

Teresa nodded.

"Sure. I'll be in my office."

What was she running from anyway? She couldn't help feel that the Lord had put her here in Stockington Falls at this point in her life for a reason. As she unlocked her office door again and dropped her purse on the desk, she decided she was being foolish.

A knock on her door had her lifting her head. It was Dennis.

"I saw you breeze by my office with your coat on. You're still coming to the community center with me this afternoon, aren't you?"

She'd forgotten. She forced a smile. "Yes, I'll be there. I wouldn't miss it, but I'm going to chat with Cammie first."

Dennis smiled and nodded. "Good. I'll see you later then."

"Okay."

Teresa barely had enough time to hang up her jacket back up on the coat hook and sit down when Cammie walked through the door and sat down in the seat opposite the desk.

"I keep telling Dennis these chairs are the most uncomfortable things in the world. I think

he ordered them at a going-out-of-business sale."
Cammie laughed. Then her shoulders lifted and
sagged on a heavy sigh. "So, what is it that you
want to talk to me about?"

"How are you doing?" Teresa asked.

Cammie stiffened. "Fine. As well as anyone can
do."

"Molly was your best friend from, what, kin-
dergarten or first grade?"

"Actually, I think it was before that. Our mothers
knew each other before we were even born. Why
do you ask?"

"You knew Molly very well. I'm guessing you
also know her husband, John, and Drew."

"They're family to me."

"Look, I don't want to cause you any pain, and
you don't have to talk about anything you don't
want to talk about."

"I appreciate that. So what is it that you *do* want
to know?"

It was clear by Cammie's impatient tone that
she wanted the conversation over with as quickly
as possible. Teresa cut to the chase.

"Can you tell me about Molly and how she was
as a mother?"

Cammie's smile was bittersweet. "She was the
best. She loved Drew so much. She and John had
a hard time conceiving, so when she finally got

pregnant with Drew she called him her special gift from God. And he was. He's a wonderful little boy. She'd do—did—anything for him."

"And John?"

Cammie's face changed. "You'll have to talk to him."

Curious, Teresa asked, "Why? Are you uncomfortable talking about John?"

"No. Like I said, he's like family. But if you want to know about how things were going with John and Molly, you'll have to talk with him directly. I won't gossip—especially since Molly is not here to tell her side."

Her interest piqued, Teresa leaned back in her chair.

"I wasn't asking about whether they were getting along. I wanted to know about him as a father, for Drew's sake now that Molly is gone."

Cammie's face showed surprise and remorse at her admission. "Oh, I thought you were asking about the rumors."

Teresa was surprised to hear that there were rumors going around about the Petersons' marriage—but that really wasn't the information she needed here. She was a child psychologist, not a marriage counselor. Drew's well-being was her concern. "No, I had no idea. It's none of my business unless it has to do with what I'm working on here. I share your sentiment. Gossip isn't something I'm fond of."

Guilt clouded Cammie's eyes, and she looked away.

"You haven't broken any confidences, Cammie. Everything you tell me is confidential."

Tears welled up in Cammie's eyes. "Why is all this important? John is a great father. I know he'll take care of Drew and love him. If Drew needs anything, John would move a mountain to get it for him. He's not like Frank Dulton."

Teresa broached the subject as delicately as she could. "Mac doesn't think that Drew had his seat belt on in the Bronco the night of the accident."

Cammie shook her head vehemently. "Impossible. Molly would never allow him in the car without the seat belt. She always made sure Drew was secured in. She used to sit in the backseat of the car with Drew when he was an infant when John was driving so she could see Drew's face when he was too small to ride in a car seat facing front. She just wouldn't drive without him buckled in."

"Mac thinks he was thrown from the car."

"He told me as much." Cammie's lips thinned. "This time Mac is wrong."

"How can you be so sure?"

"I told him the same thing that I'm telling you. There has to be another explanation of how Drew got out of the car. The injury to his arm could have happened any number of ways. He could have unbelted himself and fell, then climbed out of the car on his own."

Teresa shook her head. "But his clothes weren't wet, were they? Do you remember him being wet when he was brought in that night?"

She thought a second, rubbing her temple with her fingers. "No. He was cold but not wet. I would have remembered that. Hypothermia would have been the first thing I checked. But again, what you're implying is impossible. There's no way Molly would have had Drew in the car with her if he wasn't belted in—especially on a night like New Year's Eve. The weather was horrible. Molly hated driving in the snow."

"That brings me to New Year's Eve. What *was* she doing up on the mountain without John? You'd think that on New Year's Eve of all nights she'd be with her husband. But Dennis said you called John at home after Molly and Drew were brought in. They lived on the other side of Stockington Falls, just down the road from Dennis. Dennis said she was briefly at the party."

With a controlled breath, Cammie said, "I told you. You'll have to talk to John about that." Cammie stood. "Teresa, it's only been a few days since I buried the best friend I've ever had. I'm not sure I'm ever going to get over losing Molly. So as you can imagine these past few weeks have been very hard."

"I can. And I'm sorry I'm putting you through all this. I'm just trying to piece together the accident so I can help Benny and Drew."

She nodded. "I understand. But I really can't help you anymore. I'm sorry."

Cammie made her way to the door and then paused as if she was thinking back to the past. "Did you ask Benny how he got so wet?"

"Benny?" Teresa repeated. "Yes, he said he was looking for Chuck in the snow after he'd been thrown from the car. Benny didn't know which direction Chuck had gone. He was a little disoriented. The tree he hit was on the other side of the river. He said he searched for Chuck around the bank of the river until the heat from the burning Bronco became too hot. Then he found Chuck several yards away against another tree."

"Are you sure? You may want to ask him again." And then Cammie strode through the office door.

Teresa rose from her chair, but Cammie was already gone. Within seconds, Dennis was at her door, his face etched with worry.

"She looks really upset."

"She'll be fine," Teresa said quietly. "In time."

She wanted to believe that was true. She only wished she could convince herself of it.

"I'm almost done here. Do you want to drive over to the community center together?" Dennis asked.

"No," she said quietly. "I have an important stop I need to make before I go."

And it was a stop that was long overdue. She only hoped that she was ready.

Teresa had passed the church in town many times since she'd been in Stockington Falls. Something deep inside had always pulled her eyes toward it as she drove by, but she never stopped. Today was different. With the community center located right next door, it seemed like it was time. She felt as though she was in a stalemate where Benny was concerned. She needed clarity and there had never been a place that had helped her get clarity more than church.

It had been over two months since Teresa had sat inside any church. Her faith in God had always been strong growing up. She knew she didn't have to be inside a church to feel God's love and presence in her life. He'd hear her prayer wherever she was. Still, it had taken Teresa this long to take her first step back.

The congregational church set close to the road

near the community center was tiny in comparison to Teresa's church back in Hartford. The tall white steeple wasn't made of granite or marble. It was constructed of wooden planks and beams. The front door was small but inviting. Simple and functional. There was nothing but comfort inside those walls, Teresa told herself as she made her way up the steps.

Then why do I feel so scared?

She had nothing to fear here. And yet, as Teresa touched the front door and began to open it, she wrenched her hand back. And then the reason hit her. Although she knew the Lord would always be there for her, since Mariah's death Teresa hadn't felt worthy of His love. She didn't feel worthy enough to sit in His home.

She'd failed Him when she'd failed Mariah. And until she made that right, it would always pain her to call on His grace.

Her heart ached just thinking about it. But the realization that those were her thoughts alone became glaringly obvious to her as she stepped through the doors and walked inside. None of the judgment she feared met her here. Only love. The church was empty, yet she felt an overwhelming amount of love wrap around her.

She'd been wrong to stay away for so long. It was she alone who'd been judging her wrongs, not the Lord. It was only in seeing how harshly Benny judged himself that she realized the error of her own ways.

As she took a seat midway up the aisle and settled back, her eyes filled with tears. The Lord didn't judge the way she did. He was forgiving. It was time she stopped beating herself up and instead remembered the good she'd been able to do in the past.

She'd made a mistake. And it was a big one. If this was anyone else, she'd be telling them to accept the failure, learn from it and move on. If God could forgive her, if she could sit in His home and feel His love and grace surrounding her, then she owed it to herself and Mariah to get herself back on track. And even if she never counseled another child when she finally left Stockington Falls, she owed it to Benny to use the gift God had given her to help him heal.

Chapter Thirteen

Teresa let the cold air seep through her jacket as she walked over from the church parking lot to the community center. The sun had felt nice on her face earlier, but as the sun set, the temperature dropped and the wind that had been calm chilled her to the bone.

After her visit to the church, she'd sat in her car and had a good cry. She'd needed the release and was glad there was no one around to see her breakdown. Especially Dennis. The last thing she wanted was for him to add worrying about her onto his already-troubled shoulders. Benny and his sister's troubles were enough.

The distraction of the activity in the community center would be good for her, she reasoned. Located close to the church in Stockington Falls, the community center was a far cry from the one she was used to visiting in Hartford. The most striking difference was that it was more inviting, despite its smaller size.

As she opened the door, the sound of teenagers' chatter, laughter and life drew her in and immediately lifted her mood. The number of teenagers at the center was also telling.

It amazed Teresa there were about the same number of kids here that she'd see on a normal afternoon in Hartford, yet Stockington Falls had a fraction of the population.

Someone was doing something right by getting these kids involved. Teresa couldn't help but wonder why Benny wasn't responding to such a positive program. Was it just the friction between him and his father?

"I was beginning to think you weren't going to come. I'm glad you made it though," Dennis said, bouncing a basketball from one hand to the next as he came toward her. "We were just getting ready to get started."

"I got a little hung up. Has Benny showed?"

"He's in the locker room changing into sweats." Looking at her intently, Dennis asked, "What is it?"

"Just a thought. There are so many kids here. I'm wondering how the center manages to fill this place."

"Pastor Balinski promotes the center pretty

regularly during services, and he does a lot to get the kids motivated to come. They hold dances here every other Saturday. It keeps most of the kids occupied."

"Was there a dance here on New Year's Eve?"

"Yes, Benny was here when Chuck called him for a ride."

She nodded.

Dennis continued. "It helps that the center is walking distance from the high school, too. The location does make it easier for kids to get here and for parents to pick kids up on their way home from work."

The sound of bouncing baskets from the other teenagers as they practiced their hand at sinking hoops jarred her. "Does the high school team play here, too?"

"No, they have their own gym. Here we play strictly for fun. No set teams and no hard-and-fast rules." He made a quick turn to survey the gym. "If we have a big crowd like today we split into teams. But sometimes there are only a few kids, and I lead them in a little one-on-one."

"What about Benny? Is he up to playing?"

Dennis shook his head. "I already talked to him about his limitations for now. He can shoot some baskets but only if it doesn't hurt too much to raise his arms. I'm sure his arm is still a little stiff, so working the muscles will be good. It's really too soon for him to be running on the court with the rest of the group. I don't want to risk him getting injured further while he's still healing that shoulder."

Dennis turned and blew his whistle when he saw Benny and a few others come out of the locker room.

"If you just got here, start with a warm-up and shoot some baskets before we start the game."

Right away Teresa could see this was the last place Benny wanted to be. Not only were his shoulders sagging but he looked as if he was dragging his feet as he walked. This had nothing to do with his shoulder injury. He just didn't want to be here.

As he walked, he cast his eyes low and looked from side to side at the other boys as they gathered around. None of them treated him any different than how they treated each other, but it was clear Benny felt a little paranoia.

"Hey," he said to one kid, who lifted his hand and slapped Benny's in a handshake.

"Looking good."

"Better, anyway."

Teresa watched as Benny thrust his hands in his sweatpants pockets, wincing at the pain in his shoulder from the abrupt movement. Still, the acceptance of the other teen had obviously lifted Benny's mood. He took the basketball from his friend and got in position to shoot a basket.

She'd watch him, see how he interacted with the rest of the boys. But she couldn't help but watch Dennis with the teens, too. Dennis seemed to be a natural, one of them. And they accepted him that way.

In Hartford, many of the teens were wary of adult authority. They'd seen enough to make them distrustful of adults, but they still needed and even wanted direction, even if they didn't know it. She wondered how Dennis would fit in there. There were many strong role models for kids in Hartford. Teresa had been fortunate enough to work with many of them and had seen firsthand the good that could be done on a child's behalf.

But Dennis…he had a way with these kids. They didn't just listen to him. They admired him. That was rare.

Dennis blew the whistle one more time, and the boys moved quicker to form a group under one of the baskets.

"Not bad out there, Lambert. I don't think you missed a single shot."

The teen answered with the cocky attitude suggestive of larger-than-life confidence. "You know how it is. Just comes naturally, doc. Want me to teach you a few moves?"

The jeers from the boys echoed in the gym as they laughed.

"Modest as ever, I see," Dennis teased. "Let's tone it down a bit, though. All that sunshine you're throwing my way is blinding me."

The boys laughed again, and Teresa couldn't help but chuckle herself. The kid called Lambert grinned smugly. "I'll get you my old man's sunglasses. How about that?"

Dennis chuckled then got down to business.

"I want to introduce you all to Ms. Morales. She works with kids in Hartford, and she's new to Stockington Falls. I invited her here today to watch us play, so I hope you'll make her feel welcome."

He talked as if she'd made a permanent move to Vermont when in truth she was really just staying for a little while more. The sublease on her condo was up in the first week of March.

A few of the boys waved or said a shy hello. Most didn't pay her any attention and began circling under the basketball hoop, dribbling the ball.

"She playing, too?" Benny asked.

Dennis squared Benny with a sharp eye. "Why don't you ask her if 'she' is playing. The rest of you can break out into teams so we can start."

Teresa stifled a smile as Benny looked at her.

"It's okay, Benny. I'm going to sit it out and just watch today."

His shoulders lowered just a notch, apparently with relief.

"Hey, Uncle Den," he called out. Dennis turned. With a swift motion, Benny snatched the ball from Dennis's hands and quickly dribbled in the opposite direction as if he'd just snatched a prize.

Laughing, the two of them wrestled to get control of the ball until they were standing with the rest of the boys already split up in teams. Benny winced and then dropped the ball, rubbing his shoulder.

"Okay?" Dennis asked.

"Yeah, it's cool."

Teresa walked over to the bleachers and climbed to the third row and sat down. Being just a little higher than floor level would keep her out of the way of any stray basketballs that might get too close to the sideline.

There was a time she'd happily pop her head into the gym just to say a quick hello to some of the students before they practiced. Someone was always running over to her to tell her some little tidbit about a boyfriend or college they'd just been accepted to.

But today felt strange. Except for Benny, she

didn't know these boys. No one was rushing up to her, least of all Benny.

They were rushing to Dennis, though. The way he interacted with the boys was telling. He was good with them. They listened and responded to his coaching.

Dragging her gaze away from the boys, she glanced at the gym and saw two girls come out of the girls' locker room. Her attention was almost immediately pulled back to the basketball court by harsh raised voices.

Benny slammed the ball on the ground and let it bounce away. "You take that back," he insisted.

"No, you killed her and there is nothing you can say that's going to change that," said a boy who looked to be about the same age as Benny, slamming the ball on the ground, mimicking Benny's reaction to the confrontation. The ball bounced so hard that it flew over Benny's head and crashed into the bleachers.

Teresa snapped her attention to Benny, whose face had turned hard, and raced down the bleachers to the floor. She kept enough distance so Dennis could intervene. He was a mentor to these kids. If anyone could help defuse the situation, he could.

"Easy, Mason. I know you're upset, but no one killed anyone," Dennis interjected. "What happened on the bridge was a tragic accident."

"You're just saying that because Benny's part of your family." Mason didn't let up. His face was red, showing his anger, but he kept his body in control by keeping his distance. "But Molly Peterson was my mom's cousin. She was family, too. And now Drew has no mother."

"I'm sorry to hear that," Dennis said. "I'm sure it's been hard on your family. It's really difficult to lose someone you love."

"He did it." Mason pointed a finger at Benny. "You made her car go into the river. She's dead because of you. I saw you that night. You were probably drunk."

Teresa stepped forward into the crowd and was ready to interject until a boy from the back of the group said, "Benny wasn't drunk." The boy took a few steps forward. "Mason, you know he wasn't. You saw him here at the center right before the accident, just like I did."

Benny looked as if he was hanging on by a thread. His jaw was tight, and his eyes were cold and hard. "I didn't make Mrs. Peterson's car go off the road, either. It was already in the water when I got there. It was probably those kids playing chicken on the bridge."

Dennis placed a hand on Benny's shoulders in an effort to give him support.

Teresa asked, "What is this about playing chicken?"

The boy who'd spoken up in Benny's defense explained. "There are some kids who play chicken on the bridges. Who can make it to the bridge first, you know? They shut their lights off and drive, and whoever has the guts to keep going and make it through the opening of the bridge first wins."

"It wasn't me. I wasn't playing chicken. I was just driving Chuck home from work. Mrs. Peterson was already in the water. I heard the kid crying, too."

Teresa asked, "Benny, did someone from one of the other cars stop to see if Molly was okay? Did they help Drew get out of the Bronco?"

Benny shook his head. "They didn't do anything to help. I got to the bridge and saw the hole, saw the Bronco down in the water. I was gonna pull over and see if I could help, but then the stupid truck did a U-turn and started coming back through the bridge again. The driver was going too fast, and there wasn't enough room. It was too late for me to do anything. I couldn't right the car after I swerved to miss him. The car started to spin, and that's when I hit the tree. Chuck flew right through the windshield because he wasn't wearing his seat belt."

"That's when you went looking for him in

the snow?" Teresa asked. "Isn't that what you told me?"

"I didn't know which way he went. All I knew was he wasn't in the car anymore, and the water was right there. I heard crying coming from the river, so I went in and saw the kid strapped in the car. I don't know. I didn't want him to fall out and drown, so I took him to the bank of the river. I was going to go back and help Mrs. Peterson, but my shoulder hurt so bad and I was freezing. I just wanted to get out of the water. I felt like I couldn't catch my breath anymore."

"You got Drew out of the Bronco with a broken collarbone, Benny. You must have been in some serious pain," Dennis said. "I'm amazed you were able to carry Drew."

Tears filled Benny's eyes, and he turned slightly away from the crowd of boys who were listening to what was happening.

He turned to Mason. "I didn't mean to leave her in the car. But before I could catch my breath, the car blew up. The sky got so bright, and it got hot. I could see on the other side of the river that Chuck was just lying there in the snow. I didn't know if he was dead or alive."

"So you went to him and stayed there until the EMTs arrived," Teresa said.

Benny nodded.

Teresa glanced at Dennis and knew exactly what he was thinking. The situation could have turned out far worse than it had. The water had been rushing in the river. Being injured, Benny could have easily lost his strength and been swept under, taking Drew along with him. Then there would have been three fatalities that night instead of one.

"I'm proud of you, Benny. You did a brave thing and saved Drew's life. It's sad that Molly died, but it would have been even sadder if John Peterson lost both his wife and his son. Isn't that right, Mason?"

Mason wasn't quick to turn. Teresa sensed that he was more embarrassed by his overreaction to Benny now that he knew what Benny had revealed was the truth. But when the other boys all showed admiration for what Benny had done, he finally conceded. "Yeah, thanks."

Unsure of how to react or what to say, Benny just shrugged.

"Look, I can see we all have a little energy to burn today," Dennis said. "Why don't we skip the game and just shoot some hoops for about thirty minutes. We can get ourselves good and hungry and then get a pizza across the street. My treat."

The boys looked at each other. Some were immediately pleased with the idea and started whooping and clapping. Benny and Mason took a little longer to be won over but finally nodded.

"I can't play though cuz my shoulder is still sore," Benny said.

Dennis scrubbed a hand over Benny's head. "There's a doctor in the house. Do the best you can, and you can sit out when it starts to hurt."

Dennis tossed Benny the ball, which he caught chest center with both hands. Either he was too angry to feel any pain or his shoulder wasn't as bad as he was claiming.

When the boys were busy on the court, Teresa turned to Dennis. "That could have gone badly. But believe it or not, this was good for Benny. He needed to get that out of his system. It helps that the other kids were quick to realize that what he did saved Drew's life. Maybe they'll help him work past his guilt for not doing more." She shook her head. "All this time I've been thinking it was Chuck that Benny was suffering over."

"You think he was really feeling guilty about not being able to get Molly out of the Bronco before it exploded?" Dennis said.

"Logically, Benny has to know that it would have been a tall order for anyone to save Molly. Even if he had pulled her out, it might have been too late. We have no way of knowing if she even survived the initial crash. But it could be what has been eating at Benny. Now that he's been able to get that off his chest, I hope he opens up a little more."

Dennis turned away from the teens shooting baskets and lowered his voice so he wouldn't be overheard. "As big as Benny is, he wasn't strong enough to be in the water that night, especially after a car accident. When I think of what could have happened... I can't imagine my sister and Frank losing him. I'm proud of Benny, though. I think Karen and Frank need to know what really happened that night."

"I think you're right. Give me some time to talk with Benny, though. It may be good for them to hear it from Benny himself. But don't interrupt him now. He looks good out there on the court with the other boys. If he gets tired and sits out, I'll have a talk with him before we go for pizza."

Teresa walked over to the bench and sat down, unable to keep from feeling the smile on her face. She hadn't been the one to pull this information out of Benny. The altercation with Mason had done that. But she wasn't going to question the how or who.

It didn't really matter how it happened. They'd made progress today, and it gave her a measure of hope. The breakthrough Benny had was something they both could build on.

* * *

"I should have you come out to Hartford and work with the kids there. I think they would love you."

The lines between Dennis's brows deepened, and his expression changed from one of quiet contentment to disappointment. The change was barely noticeable. But in these past weeks, Teresa had begun to notice these subtle changes.

"I'm needed here," he said. "It's just as important for me to do good for this community as anywhere else."

"Of course it is. I wasn't implying that you should leave Stockington Falls. I just couldn't help but notice how the boys respond to you. You've got an amazing way with them. We need someone like you in Hartford."

Clearly still uncomfortable with the conversation, Dennis shifted slightly in his seat and glanced at the boys who were all engrossed in conversation and typical teenage laughter.

"I'm sure Hartford has its share of bachelor doctors who could lend a hand."

She smiled. "It doesn't have you."

"No." Dennis cleared his throat, a sure sign he wanted to move away from the subject. "I saw you sitting with Benny for a while."

She nodded, motioning with her head to where

the boys were sitting. "He didn't say anything more, but he seems to be doing okay."

"Good. Karen will be relieved."

"It was a step, Dennis. A good one but still only a step. He has to want to continue and work through his feelings."

"I know. What about you?" he asked.

"What about me?"

Dennis leaned forward and spoke quietly. "You spend your days worrying about Benny and helping him dig for the root of his troubles and yet you ignore your own."

"I'm not ignoring anything."

"Teresa, you're talking to *me*. I'm not some stranger, and I'm not one of the kids you're trying to save." He drew in a slow breath. "I've been waiting for you to talk to me."

She shook her head. "We talk all the time."

"Yeah, we talk about Benny and my sister and my work and the weather. We don't talk about what is important. Not about what's eating you up inside."

Teresa glanced at the boys. None of them had noticed the slight rise in Dennis's tone.

"This isn't the place, Dennis," she whispered.

"Is there going to be a time or a place? I need to know what happened to hurt you so badly."

"Why?"

"Because I care a great deal about you."

She closed her eyes for a brief moment as his words sank in. She knew Dennis cared. But his eyes said so much more. They echoed what she felt herself.

She'd never met a man like Dennis Harrington before. And if she was going to be at all honest with herself, she'd have to admit she wanted their relationship to grow and become more permanent.

"I don't know what you want from me, Dennis," she said.

He straightened in the chair. "Well, if that's true, then I really can't tell you. You're going to have to figure it out for yourself."

"You know I care about you."

His mouth lifted just a notch to show a half smile. "I sorta hoped that's what you were feeling."

Cocking her head to one side, she threw him a wry grin.

Dennis chuckled, but his smile quickly faded. "We've spent a lot of time together, Teresa. I could see us moving toward having a relationship—something important. But we can only go so far if you hold everything about yourself inside."

Frustrated, Teresa sat back. "Dennis, let's be honest. I'm not going to be in Stockington Falls forever. This was never supposed to be a permanent thing."

"Why not? It could be." His face grew serious, and his eyes were filled with emotion so deep that she wanted to drown in them. "I'd like it to be permanent."

"But…"

He sighed. "I can't be the only one opening up."

"I want to have more of a relationship with you, Dennis. Stockington Falls and Hartford aren't a million miles away. But I just don't know if I have it in me to give you what you want."

"Just trust me. The rest will come."

Trust. Too many people had trusted her before.

"We have another month together before my tenant vacates my condo in Hartford. Why don't we just see where this takes us?"

Dennis nodded. "I guess I'll just have to be satisfied with that. For now."

When they left the pizza restaurant and walked to their own vehicles, Teresa could tell that Dennis wasn't satisfied with her answer. She wasn't sure she was satisfied, herself.

She knew what Dennis wanted, but as the days went by, it became increasingly clear that her barriers were going to be much harder to break down than Benny's.

Unable to think of anything but Dennis, she

watched the taillights of his SUV as they drove home separately.

Home. *Lord, when did I begin to think of Stockington Falls as home?* And what was going to happen when March came and she was forced to decide whether to go back to Hartford and face her demons or stay here in Stockington Falls with Dennis?

Suddenly March seemed like it was going to come much too soon.

Chapter Fourteen

Benny's breakthrough during the basketball game had been enormous for him. While it hadn't created a flood, the little trickles of information he revealed over the past three weeks since then had been the foundation of a major change in his outlook. He seemed like a different person than the boy she'd met on New Year's Day.

Where Benny thrived, Teresa only felt more confusion over her own feelings. Dennis hadn't pressed her again about what had happened in Hartford to make her run to Stockington Falls. He seemed content to sit in the evenings by the fire or watch a comedy on television together.

But she knew he was far from content. Even though the words were unspoken, she knew Dennis wanted more than she was ready to give. He wanted a relationship, and she had to admit they'd been moving in that direction from the start. But he also wanted to talk about Hartford. She'd offered him general information but nothing that brought the conversation anywhere near Mariah and Teresa's reason for leaving. Every so often Teresa wondered if his frustration over her silence on that one point would bubble over and ruin the budding relationship they shared.

Their relationship *had* grown into a somewhat comfortable groove that she enjoyed. No longer needing to weigh their words, they spent long evenings talking about everything except what was on both their minds. *When was she leaving Stockington Falls?*

Today's news had solidified a date and left Teresa with some decisions she hadn't wanted to make just yet. The coworker who had been subletting her apartment had called to let her know that she was moving out the third week of February, having been successful in bumping up the closing date on her new house. That meant Teresa could go back to Hartford in as little as next week.

It had been easy to push away the mistakes of her past when she was tucked away in a remote mountain community that seemed light-years away from her existence in Hartford. No one was tearing into her office. There were no late-night calls. Her only concern was Benny and convincing him that the course of his life lay with his decisions and not with his father's words. She continued to urge him to look to what the future could mean if he sought continued professional help.

Now that Benny's friend was out of his coma, Chuck had come back strong, surprising everyone as his condition continued to improve on a daily basis. Weekly visits to St. Johnsbury to visit Chuck and seeing Drew bouncing back when Benny happened to catch him with Cammie at the clinic had helped lift some of the guilt from Benny's conscience. That was a blessing.

When Teresa had seen Benny today, he'd actually looked like a normal everyday seventeen-year-old. He'd begun talking about the future. Knowing the concept of having a future didn't mean that his thoughts of despair or suicide were necessarily gone for good, Teresa was guarded. But it was a clear step in the right direction toward recovery. Still, it was easy to feel good about the work she'd done with him.

Teresa couldn't be Benny's recovery, though. And Dennis couldn't be hers, no matter how much he tried to help her open up about Mariah.

However easy it was to stay cocooned in Dennis's world, pushing away the pain of what happened in Hartford aside, it would do no good. She could only move forward if she was ready to deal with the past.

Lord, that's a lot easier said than done.

As she drove back to Dennis's cottage, she mulled her next step in her mind. It was snowing again, and the snapping of the windshield wipers seemed to echo her thoughts. She hated psycho-analyzing herself. She wondered if all the kids who came to see her felt the same way.

As she pulled onto Abbey Road toward the bridge, she turned up the speed on the windshield wipers against the increasing snow and ice crystals that impaired her view. When was it ever not snowing in Stockington Falls? Her midsize sedan, while completely tuned and winterized for driving in Hartford, was all but useless on the snowy mountain roads of Stockington Falls.

Dennis had warned her that February was a brutal month in this part of Vermont. On more than one occasion, he checked the antifreeze in her car. It had become a ritual, really. Before she left the house each day, he would always ask if her cell phone was charged and if she still had an extra wool blanket, mittens and scarf in the car, just in case she slid into a snowbank and couldn't get the car out.

Teresa smiled remembering it. She liked some-one taking care of her. Never having married, she'd spent her postcollege years either living with a female roommate or, these last years, alone. She liked the feel of having a man around. And the idea of having a long-term relationship with Dennis was appealing. She'd even caught herself daydreaming about one day leaving this little cottage and moving into his house. She'd thought of things she hadn't allowed herself to think of before. Marriage and children were all at the heart of it, along with Dennis Harrington.

But she was getting ahead of herself. Although nights sitting by the fire sharing a bowl of popcorn and some conversation were comforting, Dennis hadn't asked her to stay in Stockington Falls and he certainly hadn't asked her to marry him.

She had a quick lunch at the lodge with Vanessa Kaufmann for the first time in weeks. She listened to the latest bit of gossip, but even Vanessa could tell her mind was not on the conversation. She was somewhere else.

Maybe Dennis was right. *I can do all things through Christ which strengtheneth me.*

Teresa hadn't stepped back into church since the first day she'd gone to the community center. It was time she mustered up some courage and sought counsel where she knew she'd find strength. With the Lord.

Slow days at the clinic were an unexpected gift during the winter months, Dennis thought. Ski season was still going strong and would be for a few more weeks before the weather started turning. Through the spring and the summer, the clinic would cater mostly to the locals and the occasional tourist. It would give him more time to spend with his family and with Teresa.

When he heard the knock on his door, his heart lifted just a notch.

"I know you love me, Dennis. But I know that smile isn't for me," Karen said, giving him a teasing glare.

"Come on in. I'm happy to see you." And he was. He couldn't remember the last time he'd seen his sister looking like she'd actually slept through the night without worry.

"I just wanted to pop in and thank you."

Confused, he said, "For what? I didn't do anything."

Karen rolled her eyes. "Teresa? I know it was you who got her to stay on in Stockington Falls for Benny's sake. He's like a different kid."

"I know. I'm thrilled at how well he's done."

"Frank is coming around. I think he finally sees how much Benny was in crisis, and he's agreed that we should begin having Benny see a counselor in St. Johnsbury. My only worry is he won't have the same rapport with the new counselor as he's had with Teresa. I'm going to miss her when she leaves next week."

He frowned. "Next week? Did she tell you she was leaving?"

By the look on his sister's face, he knew it was true. But why hadn't Teresa told him?

"She said the person staying in her condo has moved out. With Benny doing so well, there really isn't a reason for her to stay in Stockington Falls anymore." Karen eyed him knowingly.

His insides burned. *Lord, I'm not prepared to lose this woman. Not yet.* Deep down Dennis knew that Teresa would go back to Hartford and that she even *needed* to go back there. But that didn't mean he was prepared for it.

"Is there, Dennis? Is there a reason she should stay?"

His sister wasn't a stupid woman. No doubt she knew exactly how strong his feelings were for Teresa. But she never said a word or gave any hint of curiosity about it until today.

Teresa hadn't told him she was leaving.

"Apparently there isn't," he answered.

"You're angry, Dennis. What's going on?"

When Dennis had pulled into the driveway tonight, Teresa had been waiting for him on the deck of the cottage. Like normal. Dennis was starting to question what normal was for them.

Had he only been a convenient distraction? His head ached just thinking about how Karen had told him Teresa was leaving next week. It was something he should have heard from her.

Dennis turned to her, his body tall and rigid.

"I don't know. You tell me."

"How could I possibly know if you don't tell me?"

She didn't know? How could she possibly not know that Karen would have told him about the change in Benny's treatment? And the reason behind it.

Taking one step forward, the words he'd wanted to say were on the tip of his tongue, but he stopped himself. He'd given her the room she needed all along. He'd opened up his heart. Now it was her move.

Frustrated with his silence, she sighed. "You asked me to stay and help, Dennis. Well, I'm here."

"For how long?"

She shook her head as if confused, then her eyes widened with awareness. "You spoke to Karen today?"

He sighed. "Yes. When were you planning on telling me?"

Teresa looked at him directly. It gave him hope.

"In a few days. I wasn't exactly sure when I could wrap everything up at the clinic."

He nodded and grabbed his duffel bag from the backseat of the SUV.

"My staying was never about me treating Benny long-term, Dennis. You know that."

"No. But I thought our relationship had reached the point where I would, at least, hear the news from you." He turned away, wanting to walk to the house and stop this game playing. "I thought things had changed between us."

"You always knew I'd be leaving eventually, Dennis."

Anger bubbled its way up his throat. "I expected you to tell me yourself!" he lashed out, louder than he'd intended, making Teresa jump. "My mistake."

Her eyes widened. "What is upsetting you so much? Is this really just because I didn't tell you about my leaving next week? Is that it?"

"Yes," he said, his anger showing for the first time.

"But you knew I was never going to stay in Stockington Falls. I never lied to you."

He nodded in agreement. "You're right. You did tell me you were only going to stay to help Benny. I guess I was the one who foolishly misread your feelings all these weeks when we were together, while *I* thought we were building a relationship."

"You didn't misread me. You know I care for you."

"But not enough to tell me yourself about your plans to leave town. Has our relationship become another thing that you're running away from?"

"Dennis, what do you want from me?" Teresa balled her fists and stood rigid.

"I want you to be honest with me." He shrugged. "Honest about how you feel, honest about whether you want us to even try to make this work. Honest about what happened in Hartford that made you so afraid to trust yourself—as a therapist and as a woman."

She folded her arms across her chest, closing herself off again. "I'm fine. I just don't want to talk about it."

"So you say. And when you leave here you'll be able to forget about me and go on being fine. I guess there really isn't anything for us to talk about, now is there?"

She put her hands to her face and gave her head a quick shake and started to walk away. "This isn't going well. We're both a little stressed right now. Maybe I should just—"

He swung around, his frustration getting the better of him. "What? Run back to Hartford?

You're good at running, Teresa, but do you really think that's going to help?"

As soon as the words were out of his mouth, Dennis regretted saying them. It wasn't going to make either of them feel better if he allowed his frustration over Teresa's silence to build a bigger gap. When she turned back and looked at him, he saw the hurt in her eyes. But she lifted her chin and kept her emotions in check.

Just once, Dennis wished she'd allow herself to let go of her emotions. To get mad. To break down and cry. Anything to show him she'd let him in. But she didn't.

"I was going to say *go* back to the guesthouse to get my things. I have dinner plans with Vanessa tonight."

It was another slap in the face, and Dennis hated the jealousy he felt because of it. Teresa and Vanessa had become good friends. It was only fitting that they'd spend some time together before Teresa went home. But he and Teresa had been sharing dinner every evening for the past few weeks. The fact that Teresa hadn't told him about her change of plans today of all days just showed him that she was pushing farther away.

And it hurt more than he could handle.

"When is it going to stop, Teresa?" he said. "There's going to come a time when there will be no place for you to run to and you're going to have to confront your feelings about what happened. I'd like to be there when it happens. I want to be there for you."

Tears filled her eyes. "When I stop running, I'll let you know." She did an about-face and walked to the guesthouse without looking back at him.

Looking up at the big sky above, Dennis closed his eyes. In truth, he wanted to ball his fist and give a good hit to the punching bag like he used to do in the military when he'd had a hard day.

She was leaving. He hadn't been fair at all to her just now. He knew she was still afraid, and he'd pushed her too hard. That wasn't her fault.

Shooting some baskets down at the community center was sure to burn off the growing anxiety he felt, but he didn't really want the company. His mood was foul enough that it wouldn't do to subject anyone to what he was feeling. Not right now anyway. Especially when the one person he wanted to talk to, to be with, had just walked away.

He grabbed his duffel bag from the ground and headed for the house. Guilt over his actions stabbed at him. As he turned back and gazed at the closed cottage door and the drawn curtains, he chided himself for his stupidity.

She wasn't ready. Just because he longed for her to open up to him didn't mean it was something she wanted. Patience had never been his strong suit, and he was proving it now.

He loved her. He was sure of it. But he feared that love would never grow unless Teresa had it in her to open up her heart to him.

Once inside the house, Dennis dropped his bag to the floor and shrugged out of his warm jacket. Teresa had a wall up that he couldn't penetrate, and he hated it. Why was she so determined to block him out? He couldn't have been misreading her feelings for him. Was he so out of touch with women that he couldn't tell when a woman was interested?

No, he knew. When Teresa looked at him, he saw the genuine emotion in her eyes. He couldn't have been wrong about that. Did she love him? He couldn't say that for sure. But she did genuinely care for him.

And she was very good at keeping herself at arm's length. That was what drove him crazy. For a relationship to survive, they needed to trust each other with the painful parts of their lives, not just the laughter.

Teresa was a loving woman. He could see her compassion right from the start and had been drawn to it. She could talk openly and warmly about everyone else in Stockington Falls. She could ask him question after question about his deepest feelings about Benny, Donna and all the problems in his family. And truth be told, he wanted to share those feelings with her. That type of openness had been missing in his relationships in the past. It had been a shocking revelation for him as well to have someone he could share everything with.

But as their time together stretched on, it became painfully evident that she couldn't or wouldn't do the same in return.

Dennis wanted to believe it was because she was the healer and was having a hard time allowing someone else to step into that role for her. Being a doctor, he understood that well. Nurses and doctors were notorious for being lousy patients for just that reason.

Still, he knew she was hurting, even if she didn't want to admit it. She could see pain in everyone else, but he saw hers. And it pained him as much as it pained her.

What upset Dennis more was that he knew their relationship couldn't grow if that wall Teresa had erected around her heart wasn't broken down enough to let him in.

His house had always been quiet, and now it suddenly screamed silence to him. He could smell Teresa's perfume in the kitchen, still lingering in the air from when she'd been there last night. His heart ached. He already missed being with Teresa, but he'd give her some space.

Abandoning all thoughts of eating dinner, he climbed the stairs and decided to shower and busy himself with paperwork from the clinic. As he walked each step, he said a silent prayer that God would lead him in the direction he needed to go to reach Teresa or give him the strength to let her go when the time came.

He knew one thing for sure: whichever path He decided was right for Dennis wasn't going to be easy.

Chapter Fifteen

Teresa slammed the car door shut and walked up the path toward where Dennis stood. He'd been cutting wood. No doubt he'd put all his effort into it, too, judging by the look of all the wood chips and the stacked pile of logs that now sat next to him in the cart.

After yesterday's argument, nerves skittered up her spine at the thought of having another discussion about her leaving. But after rolling things over in her mind last night and praying on what the right course of action was, she finally understood why Dennis was so upset.

He placed the ax against a wide log and bent down to pick up the pieces he'd already cut. With little effort, he tossed them into a cart that already had wood stacked.

She waited until he glanced up at her.

"Back from meeting with Karen and Frank

already?" Dennis asked. "How'd things go?" To anyone on the outside, Dennis looked normal and calm. But Teresa knew he was still bothered by their argument.

"As well as can be expected," she said. "Frank was even…pleasant."

"Really?" He raised an eyebrow. "And they said that Benny agreed to go for treatment, too?"

She nodded, which immediately brought out a smile that transformed Dennis's whole face. Teresa loved it when he smiled. His built-for-serious-business look was definitely appealing, but this softer, warmer side of him was what had captured her heart from the first.

Lord, why is it so hard to take this next step? She knew what Dennis wanted from her, why he was so frustrated. She hadn't liked it, but she now understood it.

Teresa squinted as the sun shining on the snow blinded her. Dennis picked the ax back up and gave some attention to the logs on the pile that were left to be split.

She couldn't stand it anymore. And she knew she had to do something to break down this wall. It was, after all, the wall she'd created. With every slice of the ax, Teresa felt on edge. She didn't want to go inside the cottage. It was too nice a day after all the snow they'd had last night. But she couldn't think of a thing to say that wouldn't lead the conversation to a place she'd worked so hard to avoid.

Instead, Teresa bent over a fresh pile of snow and began to roll it into a tiny ball. To her dismay, each time she got the ball moving, it would split or fall apart. After the third attempt, she stood straight up and balled her fists in frustration.

Dennis's quiet snicker from across the yard had her turning to him with a mock glare. He'd been watching her, even if he was trying his best not to.

"If you think it's so easy, why don't you give it a try?"

"I've got to split some more wood."

"What, for the whole county? You must have been at this for over an hour."

"If you want to stay warm, I have to chop wood."

She propped her mittened hands on her hips. "Dennis Harrington, there's enough wood stacked in that bin and along the trees for someone to stay warm in both the house and the cottage the rest of this winter *and* all of next. You're not fooling me. Your only excuse for continuing to split wood like you are is to keep yourself distracted."

He stood and stared at her a second and then

chuckled. "If that's the case, I guess I'm not winning this battle."

"Why does there need to be one?"

"I don't know. You tell me. That's all I'm waiting for. Just tell me, Teresa."

It took everything in her not to stomp her foot like a two-year-old. *Lord, is there a reason this has to be so hard?*

A little voice in her head told her she already had the answer God would give her. *Because anything worth having is worth fighting for.*

Could Dennis understand? Yes, Dennis was a doctor, and he'd been there when people he treated died. But she doubted ever because he'd made a grave mistake. Could she claim the same?

His eyes were impossibly bright in the sunlight. He stood there looking utterly adorable with his ski jacket and plaid wool hat on his head.

Feeling playful, she bent down and fisted a clump of snow in her mitten and aimlessly tossed it at him. Dennis watched her pathetic attempt at a throw fall miserably apart before the last remains of the snow wasted away on the ground about four feet from his boots.

He lifted his head and grinned. "What was that supposed to do?"

She chuckled at her own awkwardness. She should feel foolish, but she really didn't. Making a fool of herself in front of Dennis was easy. "Okay, so it's been a while since I last threw a snowball. Cut me some slack."

In challenge, she gathered another snowball in her hands and just stood there, eyeing him. When he just smirked and looked at her, she took a step closer and tossed a second snowball. It landed on his left boot with a splat.

His gaze dropped to his snow-covered boot then lifted to Teresa. She could hardly control herself. A giggle bubbled up her throat and became uncontrollable. In a feeble effort to contain herself, she placed her mittened hands, both covered with wet snow, over her mouth.

Within moments, Dennis was laughing, too, and she knew there was no holding the giggles back any longer.

"Don't start something you're not prepared to finish," he warned her teasingly.

Straightening her spine, she propped her fists on her hips. "Are you afraid of a challenge, Dr. Harrington?"

"Never. But I like to fight fair, and I've seen just how handicapped you are with a snowball."

"Oh, those are fighting words!"

Another giggle bubbled up from her throat, and she ran through the deep snow toward the long woodpile by the trees and gathered another snowball. She turned and suddenly Dennis was gone. Checking the fresh snow for tracks, she found nothing. Her own tracks clumsily cut a path to where she was standing.

"Dennis?" Teresa's voice floated in the air. The sound of feet crunching on broken ice made her turn toward the back of the cottage. Dennis stood there with a large ball of snow in his hand.

Her heart beating faster, she tossed her snowball and ducked behind the woodpile in fear of retribution. When it didn't come, she slowly rose high enough so she could make sure Dennis was still standing where he'd been by the cottage.

When she saw him, she burst out laughing. Dennis stood a few feet away from the cottage. She'd hit a bull's-eye. A wet pack of snow had hit him square on the side of the head. The snow he'd had in his hands had fallen to the ground.

"I was keeping my best shot for when you were feeling cocky," she said.

"Remind me to never underestimate you. I'm ready for you now, though." Bending down, he gathered a big ball of snow in his hands and tightly packed it.

With his movement, Teresa spun on her heels, laughing as she raced in the other direction. She turned only when she'd shielded herself behind a big maple tree.

"Wimp," he called out, standing out in the open.

"Some people would call me smart," she called out.

The trunk of a tree wasn't the best protection.

Teresa poked her head up from behind the tree just enough to gauge Dennis's movement. The sheer joy and playfulness of Dennis's expression made her heart squeeze. Whatever tension that had been between them earlier was now gone.

"Come on, Teresa," he called out. "You chicken?"

A lone snowball flew threw the air and landed way to the left of him.

"That was a wimpy throw."

"It was not!" she countered, standing up straight, leaving herself in full view.

He chose that moment to blast her with snowballs he'd stockpiled on the side of the cottage.

Even though she hunched down and hid behind her tree to avoid the impact, he managed to get her in the shoulder. The white powder sprayed into her face and down the front of her sweater. Needing better cover, she ran and ducked behind the woodpile again.

"We're even," Dennis called out through coned hands.

She couldn't help but laugh at the fun she was having. The last time she'd engaged in a snowball fight was when she was in high school and it'd snowed during a homecoming football game. She couldn't remember the last time she'd had this much fun.

Teresa was silent. Dennis carefully stepped forward as he moved toward the log pile where he'd seen her hide. He'd be patient. Now that he'd seen this playfulness in Teresa, he wanted it to last. He'd make his move when ready.

When there was no movement from behind the woodpile, he taunted, "Had enough, Teresa?"

She remained still. The sounds of a woodchuck burrowing into a dead tree nearby and the creaking and groaning of pine trees as they swayed in the breeze were the only things he could hear. The smell of moist wood mingled with soft, wet earth. The sun beat mercilessly down on the snow around the woodpile, blinding him.

He loved days like this, and after the tension they'd both been feeling, Dennis was glad Teresa had chosen to be a little spontaneous. He liked this side of her. He loved that she could let go of what was torturing her enough to just have fun with him and enjoy the day God had bestowed upon them.

Dennis shielded his eyes with the width of his fingers and waited for Teresa to make her move.

And he knew she would. She had spunk, and he knew she wouldn't let him off this easy, especially since she'd been the one to start this snowball fight.

"Teresa?"

Silence.

Panic rose up inside him, slow at first and then growing in a crescendo when she remained quiet. Dropping the newly balled snow he had in his hand, he advanced toward the woodpile.

"Teresa?"

When she still didn't answer, his pace quickened. Had he hurt her? Certainly the impact of the snowball hadn't been enough to do any harm, but maybe she'd hit her head on a log or a rock when she ducked down. He practically lunged to the other side of the woodpile without breathing. Immediately, he saw her scrunched down, her eyes wide-open and full of mischief, and knew he'd been had. He was barely through breathing a sigh of relief when Teresa jumped to her feet and dumped a bucket of snow over his head.

"You little cheat!"

"Oh, no," she said, laughing as she ran around the opposite side of the woodpile into the yard. "All's fair in snowball fights."

"Is that so?"

"You'd better believe it."

"Well, if that's the case..." Dennis ran after her full force. The two of them proceeded to run in circles around the cottage, hiding and taking their best shots at each other, both getting doused with flying snow.

Finally winded and wet with snow, Teresa collapsed back down on the soft, cold ground, laughing uncontrollably. Tears streamed down her rosy cheeks along with melting ice crystals clinging to her skin from the snowball fight. Her laughter was infectious and took Dennis with her instantly until his stomach hurt from laughing. Dennis wanted to drink in every bit of this incredible woman.

He sank to his knees by Teresa's side and thanked God that He'd brought this special lady into his life. She rolled over to face him. Holding his hand out to her, he said, "Come on. I'll help you up. Your hair is soaking wet."

"So is yours."

"You're going to freeze."

She was leaning back on her arms now, her face dangerously close to his.

"You're the doctor. Are you going to take care of me if I do?"

"It'd be my pleasure."

Dennis held his breath, wanting just to bend his head and get a fraction closer to Teresa. He wanted to kiss her. He knew he shouldn't. It wasn't going to change anything. She still didn't trust him with her past, which meant she still wasn't ready for a relationship. That didn't mean he didn't want to kiss her with every fiber of his being.

"I can make you a mean chicken soup," he said softly, brushing her wet hair away from her face.

"Let me translate this. You mean, Cammie gave you another recipe."

He chuckled. "Actually, no. The 'making' part is me heating up the soup I'd get from Roma. She's the one who'd make it, and it's truly the best around."

"That I believe."

Teresa gazed up into his eyes, and she was so beautiful, it stole his breath away. He *was* going to kiss her. How could he not? He loved her, and that love was hard to ignore when she was looking at him this way. What he wouldn't do to just forget all the reasons why he shouldn't kiss her and just think of why he should.

When she looked up at him like he was the moon and the stars and the very earth beneath them, it didn't feel wrong. It just felt natural, as if this was the way it was supposed to be.

As Dennis bent his head and kissed Teresa softly on the lips, he realized this kind of connection had been missing from his relationships before. *Lord, why did You bring this amazing woman into my life now when there are so many hurdles left to jump?*

He quickly forgot about those hurdles. He forgot about Benny, his sister and all the things he'd filled his days with to keep away the emptiness he hadn't even understood he'd been feeling. What he had with Teresa was the very thing missing from his life. This was love. He was in love with this incredible woman in his arms.

When they parted, he looked deeply into her eyes and saw that emotion shining back at him. She cared for him, too—more than she was willing to admit. Oh, how he wished she would take that next step and just open her heart. He so wanted to take away that pain she felt and show her what kind of relationship they could have.

When Teresa was in his arms like she was now, he saw the future. Their future. It didn't really matter if it was in Stockington Falls or anywhere else as long as they were together.

Teresa reached her arm up around him, and he drew her close. There was so much that still needed to be resolved before he could think beyond today. He pulled away, and immediately her expression collapsed.

"You have no idea how much I want to kiss you again, Teresa. How much I want to be close with you."

"Is there a 'but' coming?"

He sighed. "I guess I'm selfish. I want your whole heart, not just the piece of you you're willing to share with me."

"I don't understand. I thought we were sharing."

"You know what I'm talking about."

Her expression grew dark and serious. "You already know everything you need to know."

"How do you know that?"

Her shoulders sagged. "Because you're not a stupid man, Dennis. I know you read the papers. Why do you need me to talk about it at all?"

"I don't need to know the facts. I need to hear it from you. I need you to tell me what happened and why it pains you so much. I need you to trust me."

Instead of opening up to him the way he wanted her to, she pulled herself up from the ground.

"I do trust you, Dennis. But what do you want from me? Do you want a play-by-play like we did for Benny at Abbey Bridge?"

"If it helps, yes."

She shook her head. "I'm not going there, Dennis. I messed up. That should be enough for you. Why can't we leave it at that?"

He was standing in front of her now, his face still dripping with a mixture of sweat from running and melted flakes from the snowball fight. Remnants of snow still clung to Teresa's hair and along the collar of her jacket, which was now wet.

"We're never going to be able to have a relationship if you keep closing up like this."

Tears filled her eyes. She glanced toward the cottage and said, "I'm going to go inside now and get changed."

For a lingering moment, their gazes locked. More was said in those few seconds than had been said the entire time they'd been together. With great strength, he stepped away and allowed Teresa to walk away. He wanted to follow her. But she'd made herself clear. He'd prayed for God to give him direction. He was no closer to feeling secure in his position.

Dennis stood still in the cold, wet snow, watching as Teresa pushed through the slush. As she climbed the back porch, she didn't pause at the door and turn to look at him. She just opened the glass door and walked inside, leaving him out in the cold to watch the steady stream of drops fall from the icicles lined along the roof.

Filling his lungs deeply with cold mountain air, he ran his wet, gloved hand over his face, coating more moisture on his already-wet skin from the wet glove. Looking up at the great big ocean of sky covering him, he searched for answers. *Lord, I need them fast. I wouldn't mind a helping hand here.*

He genuinely cared for Teresa and could see a life together with her. She was special. There was a rarity about Teresa that reached out and grabbed something deep inside, pulling him to her right from the start.

There was nothing more that he wanted right then than to help Teresa break through the pain that had been holding her back. It was a risk, he knew. But it was one he was willing to take if it meant that she could be happy at last.

Chapter Sixteen

The automatic floodlights went on, alerting Teresa when Dennis pulled his car into the driveway. She stoked the fire, opening the damper to give much-needed air to the stove to get it going without having a repeat of her 911 call to the Stockington Falls Fire Department. Dennis was at her door within a minute of her hearing the car door shut.

He knocked on the door before coming in, not waiting for her to respond.

"Are you already packed?" he asked, dragging his black wool scarf from his around his neck.

"Mostly. I still have a few things to get together." She drew in a nervous breath. "The fire went dead. I forgot to load the stove this morning. So it's still cold in here."

"We could have dinner over at the house. Or if you want, we could have Roma fix us something."

As Teresa gazed up at Dennis, a lump formed

in her throat and a fear she hadn't wanted to feel fully gripped her, holding her tight.

"I'm not sure that spending the evening together is such a good idea."

Hurt clouded his handsome features. "Why not? It's your last night here."

"Exactly. It's going to be hard enough leaving tomorrow without…us dragging out our goodbyes."

She sighed, fighting to keep from showing the emotion that was eating her up inside.

Dennis bent down and kissed her on the cheek. She fought against leaning into the kiss, tilting her head so that their lips would meet instead. He smelled too good, and she knew for a fact that his kisses and embraces felt way too good for her to allow them to be her undoing. She knew what she had to do. She just didn't want to do it. And being in Dennis's arms would only cloud things for her.

The tired smile on his face wilted. "I didn't think holding you a little while longer is such a bad thing."

"I'm going back to Hartford tomorrow, Dennis."

Dennis let out a slow breath and looked away resolutely. "I know."

"You've always known I would at some point, and as much as I wasn't sure I was ready to finally do it, working with Benny and seeing his courage convinced me it was important for me to go back whether I think I am ready for it or not."

"You don't sound convincing. But I know this is something you have to do. At least Hartford isn't clear across the country. It's just a few hours away."

There was hope in his eyes. He didn't want to let her go but he would. Part of her wanted him to make her stay. She'd prayed on her decision to leave. She'd gone back to the church seeking guidance. Pastor Balinski had left her with words of wisdom from the Bible: "Be of good courage, and He shall strengthen your heart, all ye that hope in the Lord."

She needed to find her strength now. But was she really ready? Even reflection and helping Benny hadn't completely convinced her. But Pastor Balinski insisted she would have to get back into her old routine and face what she feared most. She had to trust that his wisdom was right, even if it was the last thing she wanted to do.

"True enough. But…"

"But what, Teresa?" Dennis stood in front of her, his face accusing. "You keep running away. I know you want to talk to me. I can see it. But you're doing it again. You're dancing around the subject, ignoring the very thing that is causing you pain. What's going to happen when you get back to Hartford and it's all staring you in the face? How are you going to handle it then?"

"I'm not running—not this time. I stayed in Stockington Falls much longer than I planned as it is."

"And why is that?"

"Because…because Benny needed me. I couldn't just walk away from him."

"Benny." Dennis closed his eyes and clamped down on his bottom lip. "When are you going to realize you being here wasn't just about Benny?"

"You asked for my help and I stayed."

"And that's all?"

"Yes."

His dark eyes lost their entire luster in a single moment. It was the first time she'd seen Dennis look truly hurt. Concern, empathy, laughter, frustration: those were all emotions she'd shared with this man, emotions she'd brought out in him. Pain was a first, and she hated it.

She knotted her arms across her chest.

"No," she amended. "It wasn't the only reason."

"You've got this almighty wall in front of you, Teresa. I'm here for you. Tell me what happened so I can make this easier for you."

"Why is it so important to you?"

"Because it hurts you. That's why. Because I love you. And because you're using what happened as a way to keep yourself detached from us."

She sputtered, shaking her head. "You're wrong."

"Am I?"

Memories she didn't want to think about bubbled up in her mind with alarming speed. Mariah's tears over the telephone line when she'd heard David had died, her body lying limp in a bed covered with stuffed animals. A young woman in a little girl's bed. Parents' screams. An errant tear broke free and trickled down Teresa's face.

Dennis's hands were steady and sure on her shoulders. She clamped her eyes closed to hold back her emotions, to keep more memories at bay. She shook her head violently to keep the memories away. She didn't want to go there. *Why is he forcing me to remember this horror?*

"I failed…her. What more do you want to know?"

"Tell me about *her*."

"I can't!"

The grip on her shoulders tightened as she tried to pull away. But Dennis was stronger and he swung her around to face him. "Yes, you can. Do it for yourself. Do it for us."

She shook her head, pushing the nightmare away. Trying to forget Mariah and trying to forget the truth of what ultimately was her own failing.

She opened her mouth, her sobs making incoherent words. "I didn't see it. I thought I knew what was going on, what Mariah needed, but I was wrong. It was my fault. Oh, God, Mariah! I'm so sorry!"

Sobs wracked her body, and even with Dennis's arms wrapped tightly around her, Teresa's body convulsed with emotion.

"She was so beautiful, so full of life. They loved each other, and I just…I just didn't listen. I didn't see what was really going on. She cut her wrists."

"You didn't do it to her. You can't blame yourself for what she did."

"What about David? I knew he was upset when he found out Mariah was pregnant. She told me. He was so angry that he might lose his football scholarship. He'd accused her of getting pregnant on purpose just to keep him in Hartford."

"He's a young kid."

"He's dead, Dennis. They fought bitterly about the baby, and then he took off in his car. He never should have been driving in the state he was in.

He was killed instantly when his car skidded on black ice and hit a concrete pillar down the street from Mariah's house."

Dennis pulled her even closer. She wanted to hide there, but now that the dam had been opened, she felt a deluge of emotion that she couldn't hold back.

"His teammates blamed Mariah. He had a promising future. David was so well liked. They all knew about the baby and the fight. You can't keep that kind of gossip from happening. And they blamed her."

"What did they do?"

"She couldn't get away from it. They called her at all hours of the night. They texted her on the phone with horrible accusations. I knew she was upset, but I thought it was David's death. They'd been dating so long. I thought her friends would be sympathetic. I didn't know about the bullying. If I'd known, I would have…I would have taken better care to protect her. She was in such a fragile state."

"Tell me what happened?"

Teresa couldn't hold back the sobs. Her shoulders shook, and her heart ached from her release. "A few days after the funeral, she was walking home and some kids followed her. They taunted her. She went home, locked herself in her room and cut her wrist. Oh, Mariah!"

She allowed Dennis to hold her. She didn't want to leave his arms. She didn't want to ever leave him.

"You couldn't have known, Teresa," Dennis said, his mouth against her head as he spoke. "You can't see everything. This wasn't your fault."

"I'm trained to see bullying. I should have known. It was my job, and I failed her."

Her sobs continued. She held on to Dennis— unable or unwilling to let him go, she didn't quite know. She only knew that if he didn't hold her, keep the fragile fragments of herself together, she'd shatter completely. And the thought of that frightened her more than anything she'd ever known.

Dennis held on to her for what felt like an eternity, stroking her hair back away from her face, letting her bury herself in his arms.

"When are you leaving?" Dennis finally said into the silence.

She hesitated. She didn't want to think about it just yet, even though they both knew it was coming.

"In the morning."

She rested her head on his broad chest, feeling the rise and fall of it with each breath he took.

"Thank you, Dennis," she whispered.

"For what?"

"For being you." A tear trickled down her cheek and fell to her shirt. "For caring for me the way you do."

"I'm here. I'm always here, Teresa."

Thank You, God.

"You've never asked me to stay, Dennis," she said softly.

"We both know you can't. Besides, I won't make that same mistake twice."

She lifted on her side, propping herself up on her elbow for support.

"It could be different."

"It won't."

"How do you know that?"

"I asked you to stay two months ago because I wanted you to help Benny. That much is true. I also wanted to know if this attraction that draws us to each other whenever we are together was something real. And it is. But it doesn't change the fact that something happened back in Hartford that you're having a hard time dealing with. I meant what I said, Teresa. I'm in love with you, and there's nothing more I want than for you to stay here with me. But Pastor Balinski was right.

You need to go back to Hartford to resolve what happened there before we even have a chance at a life here."

He sighed. "Don't you see? You're still running, Teresa. You didn't come here for the right reasons, and you're never going to know if this is where you really want to be unless you go back to Hartford. That was a hard pill for me to swallow when I realized it the other day."

He gazed at her thoughtfully. Who knew better than him that love alone couldn't keep her in Stockington Falls? And she did love Dennis. She hadn't realized it until that very moment.

"If you really want to be alone tonight, I'll understand," Dennis said. "I don't really want to leave you alone like this. I'd like nothing better than for you to come back to the house with me and just sit with me in front of the fire while I hold you."

"I think I need some time."

He nodded but didn't say more. She knew what he wanted to hear. The words were still left unspoken.

And Teresa wanted to say those words. She wanted to tell Dennis that she loved him and that she didn't want to leave behind what they had shared. But somewhere in the back of her mind she heard a little voice of reason that told her Dennis was right. She had to leave Stockington Falls and face what she'd run from in Hartford. So instead of telling Dennis everything she felt in her heart she listened to the door close behind him.

Chapter Seventeen

The frigid cold bit at Dennis's warm skin. It was only a short walk up the shoveled path to the house, but to Dennis, it felt like he was walking in slow motion.

What was it they said about familiarity being a comfort?

All this time he'd been in Stockington Falls without Teresa, he'd been alone. Coming home from the clinic, he'd found comfort in the sameness and quiet of his life. As he opened the door and stepped into his lonely kitchen, he wondered where the comfort had gone.

After getting too little sleep, Dennis climbed down the stairs to make a pot of coffee. Filling the pot with water, he glanced out the window toward the studio and saw Teresa's bags were packed and propped just outside the guesthouse door. The sun was blinding against the snow and stinging his already-swollen eyes.

She was leaving. That much was obvious. But was it just him? Or was it Stockington Falls all together?

Now this scene was vaguely familiar to him.

He yanked the back door open and stood in the doorway in his bare feet, a pair of sweatpants and a thin cotton T-shirt. A stab of pain pierced his heart when Teresa appeared at the door, locked it and, turning his way, caught his gaze. Her eyes said it all.

"Good morning," he called out in as normal a voice as he could muster. It wouldn't help either of them to make this goodbye more difficult than it was already going to be.

She smiled weakly, her sweet face drawn with the same emotion he felt deep inside.

"Do you have time for coffee?"

She hesitated a moment before nodding. "Let me just get these bags in the trunk, and I'll be there."

The walk down the hall to change into a clean shirt and then back to pull some coffee mugs from the dishwasher felt like a dead man's walk. Teresa was leaving. And although he knew this day was inevitable, Dennis hadn't counted on falling in love with her, hadn't counted on it hurting so much.

She stood at the doorway in her coat and scarf, looking as beautiful as the day she limped into the clinic three months ago. Her dark hair fell to her shoulders and fanned out around the soft white knit of her scarf.

Lord, I'm really going to miss this woman. And he didn't want to have to. He didn't want to go back to a familiar quiet existence where he ate dinner by himself and came home to nothing but an empty house.

"Are you going to stop over and see Benny before you go?" he asked, forcing some sort of conversation into the strained silence.

"No. I've already said my goodbyes. I'll stop by the resort really quick to say goodbye to Vanessa on my way out of town, but that's all."

"She's going to miss you. Benny's going to miss you, too, you know."

"I know, but I'm confident he'll be okay now that he's agreed to go into counseling in St. Johnsbury. Last time he visited Chuck, I hooked him up with a counselor at the hospital. They seemed to hit it off well. Karen is committed to making sure Benny goes, and I think even Frank sees the difference in Benny."

"That's good news then."

She shrugged out of her coat, propped it on the back of the chair and sat opposite him at the battered oak table where they'd shared countless breakfasts and dinners. Brief as her stay was, it was going to seem odd not seeing her car parked beside his.

"We still don't know who those kids were that were playing chicken on the bridge New Year's Eve. I wish we'd found out if only to find a way to prevent someone else from getting hurt. But I can't do anything more to help clear up what happened."

"A lot of people appreciate all you've done, Teresa. You were good for us here."

"Thank you. I needed to hear that." Her voice filled with regret. "I don't want to leave here having you believe you mean nothing to me."

Raw emotion pulled behind his smile. "I think I know."

"Do you really? I don't want you to just think it, Dennis. I want you to *know* how much you mean to me."

"I know."

She sputtered. "Please don't be so 'adult' about this."

"Trust me, if I thought throwing a tantrum would help, I'd do it to keep you here. That's how much I want you to stay. But I also know you have to leave, and I don't want to make it any harder for you."

"I don't know what's going to happen back in Hartford. I'm so confused, Dennis. I don't know what you expect me to do. I... It would make it so much easier if you'd just ask me to stay."

He shook his head. "You know I can't do that. You want me to give you permission to ignore what you ran from. As much as it hurts to see you leave, I won't do that. No matter how much I love you, I know you'll always wonder if you made the right decision. You can't avoid confronting what you left behind. If you do, you may end up resenting me and leaving later when it'll hurt far worse than it does now. I've been down that road. And quite frankly, it's not one I want to travel again."

"I'm not Donna," she said tightly. "I'm not going to leave you a note and just check out."

He smiled, even though his heart ached so much he wanted to rip it out of his chest. "No, you aren't, but you do have to go back to your old life, face the things that drove you away, before you know for sure what you want and where you want to be. You have some unfinished business there. Even you know that. If you thought otherwise, you never would have packed those bags last night. If you stay now, all I'll be is your crutch."

She swiped at an errant tear on her cheek. Wordlessly, she pushed the chair away from the table and stood, leaving the untouched cups of coffee on the table.

She turned and slipped back into her coat. Her head was bent, and her silky hair fell in front of her delicate face, hiding tears he knew were there.

He wouldn't say goodbye. Anything but that. And yet, he knew she was leaving and there was a strong chance that she would never come back and that he'd never see her smiling face tilt up to look at him as he held her in his arms.

"You'll take care on the drive home?" he said.

"Yeah," she said, her voice shaky, her hands fumbling with the buttons on her jacket.

Dennis dragged Teresa into his arms, needing to hold her, needing something more than this heartbreak that was raking his insides to shreds.

He covered her mouth with his, let himself selfishly take from her what comfort he knew kissing her would bring. He loved her, and it was killing him to let her go.

Without looking at him, Teresa pulled away and walked out the door. He fought the tremendous force pulling him to watch from the frosted window as Teresa drove away.

Hartford was a long way from Stockington Falls—not just in miles but in atmosphere. Teresa had found it easy to meld into the groove she'd left over three months ago. There were sympathetic eyes and smiles from familiar faces greeting her the first few days at the high school.

Even Spencer had stopped by to see how she was doing.

"I'm back," she'd insisted.

His gray hair finally winning over his blond, Spencer had stood in the doorway of her office, his arms knotted. He wasn't buying it. But instead of telling her so, he'd just nodded his head, his smile masking his deep concern.

"What took you so long?" he'd asked.

She'd shrugged. "I got hung up."

"It happens."

Not to me, she'd thought.

That conversation had been a week ago, and her head still wasn't in Hartford, even though she was physically going through the motions. Her heart was somewhere else.

The teacher she'd been subletting her condo to had moved out the week before Teresa had returned home. But she and her husband had liked her condo so much that they'd expressed interest in purchasing it as an investment if she was considering leaving permanently.

Was she? Teresa had given the idea some serious thought. Sure, she was going through the motions here in Hartford. Students paraded in and out of her office, her life becoming a normal routine again. No one understood how she could have ever thought Mariah's death had been her fault. Logically, Teresa knew it wasn't. At least now she knew. She was a good counselor and could make a difference.

Even in Stockington Falls.

On her second week home, she curled up on her sofa with a stack of magazines from the past few months that were delivered to her P.O. Box while she was gone, intending on getting back to business. One page, and then the next and then the next, failed to hold her attention. Her mind kept wandering to cold Vermont nights and hot spiced cider as she curled up on the sofa with Dennis Harrington.

She closed her eyes and tossed the magazine to the coffee table. Even the bright colored brocade fabric she'd spent so much time choosing when she bought her living-room set suddenly seemed pale next to the memory of the overstuffed sofa Dennis had in the living room of his farmhouse.

She let out a heavy sigh. She missed Dennis. Lord, how she missed him. And she wasn't going to stop missing him by sitting in Hartford crying.

Without thought, she dragged the cordless phone from the end table and punched in a number. Vanessa Kaufmann picked up on the third ring.

"What's doing, honey?" Vanessa asked, her voice spirited as always. "It's so good to hear your voice again!"

"I'm going to need a room."

"A room, huh?"

"Just in case."

"Does this mean what I think it means? Are you coming back to Stockington Falls for good, or is this just a visit again? Either way, I'm thrilled."

Teresa smiled inwardly, a heaviness finally lifting from her heart. A lot had to happen before she could make that decision for sure, but this was a first step.

"I tell you what. You'll be the second one to know."

The clinic was quiet, Dennis thought as he finished sifting through a mountain of paperwork ready to be submitted to insurance companies. Usually medical staff did all the paperwork, but there were patient reports and dictations he had to attend to himself. Sometimes it was just easier to do the work instead of passing it off and explaining things.

It was certainly easier than going home to an empty house like he had the past few weeks. St. Patrick's Day was going to be a wild weekend. Hal and Vanessa Kaufmann were throwing a big party in celebration. Chances were a few of those partygoers would land up in the clinic for one reason or another. The clinic hadn't been that busy since New Year's Eve, and he hoped that St. Patty's Day wouldn't end up like that.

A light down the hall flicked on, drawing Dennis's attention from an insurance form.

"Forget something, Cammie?" he called out. No answer.

With the sound of footsteps echoing in the empty corridor, he pushed out from behind his desk.

"Cammie?"

He heard the door to the room diagonal from his office unlock. It was the room Teresa had used while she was working at the clinic. No one had used the room since she'd left for Hartford.

His heart slammed against his ribs as he bolted through his office door into the hallway. The door to Teresa's temporary office was ajar, and light spilled into the dim corridor. A few wide strides and he was standing in the doorway, unable to believe what his eyes were seeing.

Teresa Morales stood behind the old utilitarian desk like a mirage. Her silky hair flowed down around the shoulders of her coat. Her deep blue eyes smiled up at him, causing an electric explosion inside him.

She nonchalantly reached into the cardboard

box propped on the barren desk and pulled out a picture frame, gently placing it on the corner of the desk before uttering a word.

"Good evening, Dr. Harrington." Her voice was smooth as silk and floated to him like a whisper on the wind. "When you weren't at the farmhouse, I figured I'd find you here. You know, too many late nights can't be good for your health."

"Is that so?"

"Yes. And eating fine home cooking from Roma's by yourself is nice, but—"

"What are you doing?" he said.

She slipped out of her coat and draped it on the chair before coming around from behind the desk.

"I didn't think there was any reason to wait until tomorrow to unpack. Especially since you were still here."

He stood like stone, his mouth agape. Her expression suddenly collapsed and her smile faltered.

"I wanted to surprise you. I thought maybe I'd try to get a state grant to work part-time at the high school," she said, dragging in a deep breath and then sighing. "I should have called and told you I was coming. I just assumed… I guess I shouldn't have assumed."

He tamped down the slice of hope. "Tell me one

thing. Are you really here in Stockington Falls for good?" he asked, his voice slightly breathless.

She was here in front of him after all these weeks. All the nights he'd lain awake, memories of her haunting him, were forgotten in an instant. But if she walked out of his life again, he didn't think he could bear it.

She tossed him a wry grin, light reaching her eyes and making them spark to life again. "I figured since you didn't call, I'd just take matters into my own hands."

"I wanted to give you time to heal."

She smiled up at him and his heart squeezed. "I'm all healed, Dr. Harrington. And I know what I want. Do you still have my room back at the farmhouse?"

"The guesthouse isn't an option," he ground out, his voice harsher than he'd intended. "Not on a permanent basis anyway."

Her gaze drifted from his face to the box on the desk. She pulled out a book and dropped it on the desk with a clunk. "I understand if you need time. I reserved a room at the resort just in case—"

"Not at the resort either. I want you with me." He advanced toward her, scooping her into his arms without really knowing that he'd done it. Teresa was in his arms, and that was all that mattered.

"I know what I want, too, Teresa. I don't want to spend another day without you."

He kissed her neck, dragged in the scent of her—the soft feel of her—and felt himself go weak. He'd tried so very hard these past few weeks to rid himself of his longing for Teresa Morales, but now that she was in his arms again he couldn't deny it any longer. She felt so absolutely right, so exquisitely perfect pressed against him that something inside him finally slipped into place, and he knew without a doubt she belonged in his life forever.

"I love you, Teresa Morales. You can't know how much I've been missing you."

"I love you, too," she said against his lips, tears breaking free from her eyes.

He kissed her again, tears building behind his eyelids. How had he been so blessed for God to bring such an amazing woman into his life?

"I know you wanted to, but you were right not to ask me to stay. Although I have to admit I hated you for it that first week. I wanted to stay, and I wanted you to ask me to stay. But it wasn't fair for me to put that all on you. I realize now it was just a cop-out, another way for me to avoid what I didn't want to face. I needed to go back to Hartford to know that Mariah's death wasn't my fault. I'm good at what I do, and I love doing it. But I don't need to be in Hartford. I belong here with you."

"Are you sure? I mean, I want you to really be sure."

She nodded and wrapped her arms around his neck, leaning into his embrace. "I'm not running away from anything anymore, Dennis. I'm running *to* something I want so very much. And I'm not letting go this time."

"There might not be as much excitement for you here in Stockington Falls. Can you live with that?"

She chuckled softly against his ear. "I have a feeling our lives will be changing soon enough and we'll have all the excitement we can handle—God willing, anyway."

He gazed down into her tear-filled eyes, realizing that tears were blurring his own vision. "What do you mean?"

"Walking around the high school last week I realized that I'd been running a long time, even before Mariah's and David's deaths. And now I think I'm finally healed. There is more I want in my life. I've always thought of the kids I work with as my kids. But when I think of us, I realize I want to have a family of my own. You did say you wanted children, didn't you?"

He dug his fingers in her silky hair and kissed her lips softly. He couldn't possibly love this woman any more than he did right at that moment.

She laughed through tears. "Do I have to do all the asking, Dr. Harrington, or are you going to finally ask me?"

His laugh was rich, coming from deep within the swells of his heart and happiness. "Marry me, Teresa. Make babies with me. Be my wife, my family, my best friend. Let me love you always."

Tears spilled over the rims of her eyes and trickled down her cheeks. "There. That wasn't so bad, was it?"

"Not as long as your answer is yes."

"Yes, I will marry you, Dennis."

He wrapped her in his arms and kissed her again, vowing to never let her go. With Teresa in his arms, with the future they'd yet to share ahead of them, he knew that home would never be a lonely place. She'd come into his life needing time to heal. But winning her love, feeling it fully, had healed a lonely heart he didn't even know needed mending. And that heart was his own.

* * * * *

Dear Reader,

Like most stories, *In a Doctor's Arms* started out as a small seed of an idea. But unlike many of my other books, this story has a history.

Stockington Falls doesn't exist on any map. It's a fictitious town in Vermont that was created over ten years ago through an IM conversation with my dear friend Cathy McDavid. Our idea was to take each season and create a novella series that would span a full year. We each wrote two stories. Although the novella was never published, what came out of working on that project is an amazing friendship that I will always cherish!

"A Time to Heal" was the title of the first story I wrote for that novella series. Rather than keep that story hidden away under the bed collecting dust, I pulled it out, took another look and thought it would make a great Love Inspired romance. That novella became the bones of the story for *In a Doctor's Arms.* As I reestablished my connection with these characters from Stockington Falls, Vermont, I fell in love with Teresa and Dennis all over again. I hope you will, too!

I love hearing from readers. Please visit me and other Love Inspired authors at:

http://www.craftieladiesofromance.blogspot.com
http://www.ladiesofsuspense.blogspot.com
http://www.loveinspiredauthors.com

Many blessings,

Lisa Mondello

QUESTIONS FOR DISCUSSION

1. Raising teenagers can be difficult. Have you or someone you know had to deal with the same pressures of raising a teenager like Benny? How did you handle it?

2. Teresa finds herself confronting the very thing she fears most, counseling another teenager in trouble. Have you ever had to face something you feared that strongly? How did you overcome your fear?

3. Dennis is stuck in a difficult position. His nephew clearly needs help, but he doesn't want to pry into his sister's personal life either. How do you think Dennis handled the division of uncle versus doctor with his sister and nephew? Would you have done something different?

4. Despite falling in love with each other, Dennis knows Teresa needs to go back to Hartford and face the pain she's running from in order for them to have a chance at a real relationship. Teresa clearly wants Dennis to ask her to stay in Stockington Falls, taking

the burden of going back and facing the past off her shoulders. Do you think it was fair of her to expect this?

5. Depression issues can affect an entire family. How does Benny's depression affect his parents? His uncle?

6. Do you think Teresa was too hard on herself about Mariah's death? In what way did her experience shake her relationship with God?

7. Bullying in school can be very damaging to a child's self-esteem and leave the child depressed. Do you know of a child who has been affected by bullying at school? How did you help them deal with it?

8. How was Benny's confrontation at the community center good for him and for Teresa?

9. How did Teresa finally reconcile her guilt and her distance from her faith?

10. What is your favorite scene in *In a Doctor's Arms?* Why did that scene have an impact on you?

11. Was there any one character in *In a Doctor's Arms* that you could relate to more than the others? What did you see in that character that made you feel that way?

12. Teresa's knee-jerk reaction after Mariah's death was to run away from the pain. Have you ever run away from a problem or failure in your life? How did it make you feel to do that? How was the situation resolved?

LARGER-PRINT BOOKS!

GET 2 FREE
LARGER-PRINT NOVELS
PLUS 2 FREE
MYSTERY GIFTS

Larger-print novels are now available...

YES! Please send me 2 FREE LARGER-PRINT Love Inspired® novels and my 2 FREE mystery gifts (gifts are worth about $10). After receiving them, if I don't wish to receive any more books, I can return the shipping statement marked "cancel". If I don't cancel, I will receive 6 brand-new novels every month and be billed just $4.74 per book in the U.S. or $5.24 per book in Canada. That's a saving of at least 24% off the cover price. It's quite a bargain! Shipping and handling is just 50¢ per book in the U.S. and 75¢ per book in Canada.* I understand that accepting the 2 free books and gifts places me under no obligation to buy anything. I can always return a shipment and cancel at any time. Even if I never buy another book, the two free books and gifts are mine to keep forever.

122/322 IDN FC79

Name	(PLEASE PRINT)	

Address		Apt. #

City	State/Prov.	Zip/Postal Code

Signature (if under 18, a parent or guardian must sign)

Mail to the **Reader Service:**
IN U.S.A.: P.O. Box 1867, Buffalo, NY 14240-1867
IN CANADA: P.O. Box 609, Fort Erie, Ontario L2A 5X3

Not valid to current subscribers to Love Inspired Larger-Print books.

**Are you a current subscriber to Love Inspired books
and want to receive the larger-print edition?
Call 1-800-873-8635 or visit www.ReaderService.com.**

* Terms and prices subject to change without notice. Prices do not include applicable taxes. Sales tax applicable in N.Y. Canadian residents will be charged applicable taxes. Offer not valid in Quebec. This offer is limited to one order per household. All orders subject to credit approval. Credit or debit balances in a customer's account(s) may be offset by any other outstanding balance owed by or to the customer. Please allow 4 to 6 weeks for delivery. Offer available while quantities last.

Your Privacy—The Reader Service is committed to protecting your privacy. Our Privacy Policy is available online at www.ReaderService.com or upon request from the Reader Service.

We make a portion of our mailing list available to reputable third parties that offer products we believe may interest you. If you prefer that we not exchange your name with third parties, or if you wish to clarify or modify your communication preferences, please visit us at www.ReaderService.com/consumerschoice or write to us at Reader Service Preference Service, P.O. Box 9062, Buffalo, NY 14269. Include your complete name and address.

LILP11

Love Inspired®
SUSPENSE
RIVETING INSPIRATIONAL ROMANCE

Watch for our series of edge-
of-your-seat suspense novels.
These contemporary tales
of intrigue and romance
feature Christian characters
facing challenges to their faith...
and their lives!

AVAILABLE IN REGULAR
& LARGER-PRINT FORMATS

For exciting stories that reflect traditional values,
visit:
www.ReaderService.com